"It Can't Happen Again, Adam.

"No more little touches, no more looks, and no more kisses."

Adam gave Julia a bland I-don't-know-what-you-mean look that infuriated her.

"You know exactly what I'm talking about," she said. "You're doing it deliberately. I don't know why you're doing it, but I want you to stop. We're business colleagues working on a very important project together. That's all."

"Do you kiss all your business colleagues the way you kissed me?" he asked.

"No, of course not."

"Then I'd say we're more than just business colleagues. You're afraid."

"I don't have to justify my feelings. Why are you pursuing this, anyway?" she demanded.

"Pursuing you, you mean? Maybe because still waters run deep. You hide your light under a bushel, and I'm curious to know why."

"And I'm curious to know why you, the creativity specialist, are suddenly talking in clichés."

"You've driven me to it," he admitted readily. "See what you've done to me?"

Dear Reader:

As you can see, Silhouette Desire has a bold new cover design that we're all excited about. But while the overall look is new, two things remain the same. First, we've kept our eye-catching red border. You can be sure to always spot Silhouette Desires on the shelves! Second, between these new covers are the high-quality love stories that you've come to expect.

In addition, the MAN OF THE MONTH program continues with Mr. September, who comes from the pen of Dixie Browning. Clement Cornelius Barto is a unique hero who is sure to charm you with his unusual ways. But make no mistake, it's not just *Beginner's Luck* that makes him such a winner.

October brings you a man who's double the fun, because not only is Jody Branigan an exciting hero, he's also one of Leslie Davis Guccione's Branigan brothers. Look for his story in *Branigan's Touch*.

We at Silhouette have been happy to hear how much you've all enjoyed the Year of the Man. The responses we've received about the special covers— and to each and every one of our heroes—has been enthusiastic. Remember, there are more men ahead in 1989—don't let any of them get away!

Yours,

Lucia Macro
Senior Editor

CATHIE LINZ

ADAM'S WAY

SILHOUETTE *Desire*

Published by Silhouette Books New York

America's Publisher of Contemporary Romance

SILHOUETTE BOOKS
300 East 42nd St., New York, N.Y. 10017

ISBN: 0-373-05519-6

First Silhouette Books printing September 1989

Books by Cathie Linz

Silhouette Desire

Change of Heart #408
A Friend in Need #443
As Good as Gold #484
Adam's Way #519

CATHIE LINZ

got the idea for *Adam's Way*, her sixteenth romance, while sitting in a creativity seminar and growling like a lion! For the past eight years Cathie's been a full-time writer of contemporary romantic fiction, which is quite a change of pace from her previous career in a university law library. This Chicago-area author is an avid world traveler. Still, she's always glad to get back home to her two cats, her trusty word processor and her hidden cache of Oreo cookies!

One

***

Did I miss anything?'' Julia Trent whispered as she slid into a seat next to her friend and fellow management-seminar instructor, Maria Hidalgo.

"No, the meeting hasn't started yet," Maria whispered back.

"Good." Julia slipped her briefcase under her chair, realizing as she did so that the room was already filled to capacity. "Thanks for saving me a seat."

"No problem. What kept you?" Maria asked.

"The business-efficiency seminar I was giving ran late, *and* it was clear on the other side of the building!"

"Bad planning," Maria noted with a teasing smile.

Julia returned the smile. "Who had time to plan, badly or otherwise? This meeting was only called yesterday; there hasn't been any time to do much . . ."

"Except worry," Maria inserted.

"Worry?" Julia turned to look at her in surprise. "Why?"

"Because a meeting like this isn't called every day of the week, at least not here at Dynamics Incorporated. But then you've worked here longer than I have; you know that already."

"Usually we do have more advance notice, that's true," Julia admitted.

"And usually we know what the meeting's going to be about. It isn't left as a surprise. Everyone's been going nuts trying to figure out what's going on. You work closely with our vice president. What did Helen tell you?"

"Just that everyone was in for a pleasant surprise." Julia shrugged. "Other than that, I'm as much in the dark as you are."

"How can you stay so calm? Look around you. Everyone else is at least a little anxious and certainly very curious."

Julia had already detected a definite tension in the atmosphere—people were sitting with their backs perfectly upright, their shoulders straight—no slouching or fidgeting. Everyone was stiffly at attention, anticipating the best and fearing the worst as they waited for the meeting to begin.

"It's the uncertainty that makes people so nervous," Maria explained.

"I'm sure we'll find out soon," Julia murmured as Helen Armstrong approached the speaker's lectern at the front of the conference room.

"Now that you're all here," Helen said, "we can get down to business. I've got a wonderful surprise for you all. It's my pleasure to announce that Dynamics has pulled off quite a coup. Everyone wants him, but for the summer at least, Adam MacKenzie is ours!"

Now Julia's curiosity *was* aroused. She'd heard about Adam MacKenzie. Who hadn't? He was a leading authority on the subject of creativity. Julia leaned forward in her seat and tried to see the man Helen had just introduced, but her view was blocked by those sitting in front of her.

"I don't have to tell you that Adam has created quite a reputation for himself," Helen went on to say. "He's been called everything from a renegade to a crusader, but everyone agrees that he's a brilliant seminar leader and an expert in the exciting field of creativity and problem-solving. It is with great pleasure that we welcome him to our team here at Dynamics."

Julia applauded politely if somewhat less enthusiastically than her co-workers. Helen was right, Adam MacKenzie certainly did have *quite* a reputation. His off-the-wall teaching techniques were famous, or infamous, depending on whom you talked to. She'd heard tales of the wild antics he pulled in his seminars, the same antics that had earned him the nickname of Mad Mac.

"Adam will be working with those of you already assigned to the Intercorp account," Helen added.

Julia felt the first twinges of uneasiness. Mad Mac? Working with her on the Intercorp account? Oh, no. *Trouble ahead!* The thought flashed in her head like a roadside warning sign. As one of the four instructors assigned to the Intercorp account, Julia was certainly surprised by this news. Why hadn't Helen warned her? She leaned forward once more, determined to see what kind of man she'd be dealing with.

The person ahead of her shifted in his seat and Julia finally got a clear view. Her brown eyes widened. *This* was Adam MacKenzie? Mad Mac? He didn't look old enough to have earned such a name for himself. He also looked surprisingly normal, even fairly good-looking, if one went in for men with dark hair and rakish smiles.

Unfortunately Julia's view was abruptly cut off as the person sitting ahead of her shifted back into his original position.

"He's younger than I thought he'd be," Maria whispered. "What do you think?"

Julia shook her head. "I don't know what to think." She'd only gotten a brief glance at him, after all. Just long enough to be struck by his relative youth and seemingly normal appearance. He was wearing a dark suit, white shirt, and dark tie—one couldn't get much more conservative than that. From his reputation she'd expected something quite different, perhaps an eccentric professorial type with white hair and a rumpled appearance. Or a throwback to the hippie generation, complete with love beads and a Nehru jacket. Instead she'd seen a typical-looking businessman in his mid-to-late thirties.

Perhaps his reputation had been exaggerated. That possibility relieved her somewhat. Julia preferred predictability to wildness any day.

Her curiosity increased as Adam got up to speak. As soon as he opened his mouth, he had the audience in the palm of his hand. He had a confident presence that made others listen to what he had to say. But what he had to say was a little strange, or at least Julia thought so.

"I teach creative problem-solving," Adam announced, "but rather than tell you, I prefer to show you what I mean. I'd like everyone in the room to put your hands together, the way you did in grade school when the teacher told you to fold your hands on your desk." He waited until everyone had done what he'd requested. "Okay, now look at your hands and notice which thumb is on top, your left or your right?"

Julia looked down at her hands and wondered what this had to do with problem-solving, or creativity for that matter.

"You folded your hands the way you did without even thinking about it. It's a habit," Adam informed them. "Now I want you to switch positions and fold your hands with your other thumb on top. Sounds easy, right? Try it."

Julia did and found she couldn't get it right. Her hands wanted to go into their normal folded position, and it felt strange trying to make her fingers do otherwise.

"You see?" Adam directed a teasing smile at the audience. "It's not that easy. Why not? Because now you have to think about it. I use this example with my class as a means of showing you one way in which we stifle creativity. We are creatures of habit. People fall into certain routines, certain ways of doing things, like folding their hands, and they never try anything else. Because it's easier not to think about it, to do things the way they've always been done. But this kind of thinking blocks creativity, puts up barriers to trying new approaches. It's a small example, but it's one way to get you thinking about opening up your own avenues of creativity. Today you may be folding your hands differently, tomorrow you may be thinking differently, and then who knows what brilliant piece of problem-solving you may come up with when you're open to creativity? Somewhere out there is a better mousetrap just waiting to be made." Adam paused for one dramatic moment, then raised an eyebrow at the crowd. "And given the choice, wouldn't you rather be the creative mousetrap maker than one of the mice?"

Everyone laughed before applauding in agreement.

Everyone, that is, except Julia. Grimacing slightly she released her twisted up fingers. This pop-psychology stuff wasn't her idea of proper business-management material.

Helen stood and spoke. "As you can see from just that brief presentation, Adam is a very effective speaker, and we here at Dynamics are lucky to have him. We may not be the largest business-seminar company in Chicago yet, but our aim is to be the best, and we pride ourselves on hiring the best. Working together, we can make this company grow and prosper. Just one more thing before we conclude. I'd like those instructors already assigned to the Intercorp project to stay behind, please. Thank you."

The room emptied quickly. Julia stayed where she was and watched Adam MacKenzie, wondering how to peg him.

Adam was aware of the woman in the back row; he had been since she'd quietly slipped into the conference room. He wasn't sure what it was about her that had first caught his attention—idle curiosity at a latecomer, perhaps. But then he'd noticed how calm she was, how serene. While everyone else around her had projected nervous tension, she'd stood out like a tranquil oasis.

It was entirely unintentional on her part, he was sure. She wasn't dressed like someone who wanted to stand out. Her business suit wasn't a bold red like Helen's or a stark black like that of the woman sitting next to her. It was a blend-into-the-background beige, understated yet classy. With her shoulder-length brown hair and creamy skin, she could have been striking. Instead she looked . . . composed. Her bangs were the only touch of whimsy to an otherwise elegant appearance. She had brown eyes.

She also had nice legs, Adam noted with a quick smile.

He had a nice smile, Julia noted from the back of the conference room and then wondered uneasily just what it was that he was smiling at. It couldn't be her. Men like him didn't smile at women like her. She knew what kind of image she projected. Quiet capability.

There was nothing quiet about Adam MacKenzie. At first glance, he might look like just another businessman, but having watched him as he spoke, she knew he possessed a dynamic vitality, an intensity that created sparks. He was the type of man who made things happen.

Now that she had an unobstructed view of him, she filed away a few other facts. He was fairly tall, probably six feet; his eyes appeared to be blue, but she couldn't be sure, and his dark tie seemed to have some sort of strange pattern on it.

"Let's move closer," Maria suggested. "There's no need for us to stay at the back of the room any longer. There are only six of us in this meeting now, anyway."

Julia nodded. Taking her briefcase in hand, she followed Maria. She noted that the other two instructors assigned to the Intercorp account, Karl Schneider and Larry White, were already waiting at the front of the room. Off to one side, Adam was still talking to Helen.

"Well, what do you think of the Boy Wonder?" Karl Schneider asked in an aside as Julia and Maria joined him.

Karl taught negotiation skills and liked to brag that he'd used those skills to mediate his own divorce. Julia considered Karl to be somewhat insecure underneath all his bravado, which is why she excused his blustery style, even though it occasionally irritated her.

"I wouldn't exactly call him a boy, Karl. He's not much younger than you are," Julia pointed out.

"He's under forty, which is what counts. To get ahead in business today, you have to have made your mark by the time you're forty. Adam MacKenzie has certainly made his mark." Karl lowered his voice confidentially. "Helen was correct in saying that Dynamics had scored quite a coup by getting him for the summer. I've heard that several other companies were vying for his services. Of course, he teaches at one of Chicago's small, exclusive North Shore colleges the rest of the year, so there's a great deal of competition for the few months in the summer that he does free-lance lecturing. I wouldn't be at all surprised if the promise of having Adam MacKenzie on board didn't play a major part in us landing the Intercorp account in the first place. It *is* the largest assignment we've gotten, and a company with Intercorp's nationwide standing would be impressed by someone with Adam's reputation."

"Someone talking about my reputation?" the subject of their conversation inquired.

Julia jumped guiltily. As Karl hurriedly assured Adam that they'd discussed him in only the most complimentary terms, she took a moment to regain her composure. Now that Adam was standing only a foot away from her, she could practically feel the waves of energy emanating from him. She could also see the print on his tie.... She squinted in disbelief. Surely those couldn't be hula dancers?

She looked up and met Adam's smiling eyes head-on. She blinked and looked away. Blue, she noted hazily. His eyes were an electric blue.

The disconcerting moment was interrupted by Helen's voice. "Adam, allow me to introduce you to everyone. I'll start with Julia Trent, our efficiency specialist. She's one of the best in her field."

Adam held out his hand and noticed her slight hesitation before taking it. He was trained to notice that kind of detail. But his training had nothing to do with the other details he was noticing about Julia. Her hands were soft, her fingers long with just the slightest tinge of polish on her nails. She wore no rings and had a no-nonsense handshake. But most importantly, her dark brown eyes were filled with wariness.

Helen had told him about Julia, praised her capability and her team spirit. Helen hadn't told him that Julia was also an intriguing blend of softness and strength. He wondered if anyone else had seen past the mask Julia wore, past the capability to the vulnerability. Somehow he doubted it. He wished he had more time for speculation, but Helen was already continuing her introductions. Reluctantly he released Julia's hand.

Feeling as if she'd just come in contact with a high-voltage transformer, Julia realized her fingers were actually tingling. She looked at them in dismay. Considering Adam's dynamic presence, she'd expected the physical contact to be charged with energy, but this was ridiculous! When his fingers had closed around her hand, she'd felt the current clear down to her toes.

Vaguely aware of Helen introducing Maria as a specialist in presentation skills, Julia watched as her friend shook Adam's hand. Was Maria feeling the same jolt of electricity? Julia wondered and then reprimanded herself for the frivolous thought. Such fanciful speculation wasn't like her. Maybe she was just overtired. She certainly hadn't been getting much sleep lately. The Intercorp project had meant many extra hours of work.

Determined to put the momentary lapse behind her, Julia was glad she'd perfected the art of hiding her emotions from those around her. At least she could be confident no one else was aware of her discomfiture. Meanwhile the introductions had moved on to Karl.

"And this is Karl Schneider," Helen was telling Adam. "You met him briefly before the meeting."

"Negotiation skills, right?" Adam asked.

"Right," Karl said.

"And last, but certainly not least, is Larry White, who is making great strides in the area of team building. Which gives me a perfect lead-in for the subject of building this team. You're all going to be working together fairly closely over the next few weeks. I know that you're already familiar with each other's subjects and means of presentation, and that Adam is the unknown quantity here. But I intend to rectify that. Adam is going to be giving a creativity seminar at a local college tomorrow, and I want you all to attend it. Consider it a brief initiation, if you will, into his style of teaching."

"It won't be as long as most of my seminars are, only a two-hour presentation instead of all day, but it will give you an idea of where I'm coming from," Adam said.

Julia thought she already knew where he was coming from—somewhere out in left field! She was more concerned with where he was going, and where the entire group would be going. Together.

"Have you worked out a final itinerary yet with the people from Intercorp?" Julia asked Helen.

"Yes, I have. You'll all be starting at Intercorp's regional offices in Minneapolis, then going on to Kansas City and St. Louis before continuing on down to Dallas and Houston. I'll give you all a copy of the final itinerary tomorrow—my secretary is still typing it up. As you know, once you begin the project next week, you'll be on the road for the next six-to-seven weeks. Intercorp has regional offices in twenty-five of the fifty states and you'll be traveling to every one of those offices to provide additional instruction for their middle managers. You'll be spending approximately two days at each location, sometimes a day longer, sometimes a day shorter."

"Building up mileage on our frequent-flyer programs," Larry noted with a smile.

"You certainly will," Helen agreed. "But we've arranged for each of you to fly home on two weekends, so you won't be away from family for the entire seven weeks. You won't all be flying home on the same weekend, but each of you all will have the opportunity to return to Chicago for two weekends out of the seven."

Julia knew that Larry was particularly pleased to hear that news. With a wife and small daughter at home, he was the one family man out of the group. She wondered if Adam had anyone at home. She didn't think that he was married, but then she didn't know much about his private life. Not that Adam's marital status mattered one way or the other to her. No, the only thing that concerned her was doing a good job on this project. Reminding herself of that fact, she focused her attention on what Helen was saying.

"As you already know, this is the largest project our company has gotten to date. We hope it is only the first of many, and we're counting on you all to do your best." He-

len smiled briefly before gathering up her notes. "Now that
the introductions and the pep talk are out of the way, I'll
leave you all to fill Adam in on the details of how our team
works."

After Helen's departure, Larry was the first to speak.
"May I say on everyone's behalf that we're looking forward to working with you, Adam," he said, ever the team
player.

"Thanks, Larry, but you may want to save that speech
until after you've participated in my seminar," Adam noted
ruefully.

"I'm looking forward to it," Larry stated with the ut-
most confidence.

Julia wasn't exactly looking forward to it, but she was
determined to hide her misgivings. She could cope with
whatever Adam MacKenzie might throw her way. Surely by
now she'd perfected coping to a fine art.

"Why don't we all sit down?" Adam suggested. He
grabbed a chair, turning it around and straddled it, folding
his arms across the back of the seat. "Tell me about your-
selves."

Karl eagerly began.

Adam was a good listener; Julia was willing to grant him
that much. And he was an excellent communicator. Everything, his body language, his casual attitude, was meant to
put them at ease. And it worked on everyone except her. She
couldn't quite let down her guard around him, and she
wasn't sure why. He made her feel...uncomfortable. And
for some reason she felt that he knew it and was amused by
it.

Usually it took a great deal to throw her, but then she reminded herself that Adam was a professional curve thrower.
That's what he did—kept people on their toes by being unpredictable and unconventional. After years of practice,
there was no doubt that he'd gotten very, very good at it.
She excused her feelings of uneasiness as being nothing out

of the ordinary considering the type of man she was dealing with.

On the surface, Julia appeared as relaxed as anyone. She answered Adam's questions, asked a few of her own, and joined in the group discussion. But Adam noticed the difference. When she spoke to any one of the other instructors, she was confident and caring. But when she spoke to him, she placed an invisible wall between them, distancing herself. Oh, it was subtle, but then he'd been trained to look for the subtleties.

He was curious; he couldn't help himself. Why was she so wary of him? Was it just nervousness on her part? No, he couldn't buy that. She still radiated that calm and serenity that had first caught his attention. She just wasn't radiating it toward him, and he couldn't help wondering why.

Hoping to find out, Adam stopped her before she left.

"You're the only one who didn't look too thrilled with the prospect of having to attend my seminar," he noted.

"I *never* look thrilled," Julia replied with a composed smile.

"Why not?"

She shrugged. "It's genetic. I come from a long line of nonthrilled people."

So she had a sense of humor, he thought to himself with a grin. Good. "No thrills, huh? What a shame." He tried to sound commiserating. "It's never too late to learn, though. There must be something that excites you."

"Many things."

"Name five." His request sounded more like an order.

She frowned. "What is this? The beginning of one of your lessons?"

"Humor me. What have you got to lose?"

"Time." She pointedly looked at her watch. "I've got a class to give in exactly four minutes."

"Then talk fast."

"Five things? Okay. Ice-cream sundaes with hot-fudge sauce, alpenglow on the mountains, Tchaikovsky...." She paused for a moment.

"That's only three," he pointed out.

"I know, I know. Give me a second..." She wrinkled up her nose as she tried to think of two more. "Paintings by Monet, and reruns of *Star Trek*," she added triumphantly.

Adam was impressed. "Ah, a woman of eclectic tastes."

"And a woman who's going to be late for her next class. Goodbye, Mr. MacKenzie."

"Make it Adam, please. And it's not goodbye. I'll see you tomorrow, remember?"

"I won't forget."

"No matter how much you might want to, right?"

"I don't know where you've gotten this mistaken idea that I don't want to attend your seminar. I'm sure it will be very educational," she said truthfully. "And I'm looking forward to it," she fibbed.

"Oh, it will be educational, all right," Adam murmured after she'd gone. "And I'm looking forward to it, too!"

Two

"Julia, do you have any idea where we are?" Maria asked as Julia stopped for a red light.

"Of course I do. Larry said this was a shortcut."

"Larry is the salt of the earth, a wonderful guy, but he can't find his way out of a paper bag."

"You're exaggerating."

"Julia, the man can't tell his left from his right!"

"A lot of people have that problem."

"True enough, but you certainly don't ask them for directions. Maybe we should have all gone in one car."

"Not possible," Julia replied. "Larry still had the sheets of plywood in the back of his station wagon and Karl just bought that little sporty two seater."

"Karl and Larry could have come with us," Maria pointed out. "They'd certainly fit in your backseat."

"Maybe they don't like my driving," Julia suggested with a grin.

"Why not? You're hardly the Mario Andretti type."

"I know. That's *why* they don't like my driving. Actually I think the truth is that Karl just wanted to show off his new set of wheels to Larry."

"Sounds much more likely. Now the only thing I can't figure out is why you took this shortcut. We're going to be late," Maria predicted darkly.

"We're not going to be late. Would you just relax?"

"You know, this will be the second time you've been late for a meeting with Adam, and that's strange because normally you're *never* late. I mean you're punctual to a fault."

"I didn't know there was such a thing as being punctual to a fault," Julia returned.

"Trust me, there is such a thing, and you've got it. This recent tardiness of yours must be some sort of avoidance technique," Maria decided. "I think you're trying to avoid dealing with Adam MacKenzie."

"Maria, I hate to tell you this, but your major in psychology is showing again."

"I mean it. Don't you think it's strange that, in all the time I've known you, the only two times you've ever been late for a business occasion happen to involve a meeting with Adam? Not once, but twice?"

Julia calmly defended herself. "Yesterday I had a class to teach, which made me late to the meeting by a mere five minutes, and that was before I'd even heard of Adam."

"Come on, everyone's heard of Adam MacKenzie. At least everyone in our line of work."

"I meant that I had no idea what yesterday's meeting was going to be about, remember? No one did. So I could hardly have deliberately been avoiding something or someone I didn't even know would be there."

"Sounds like convoluted thinking to me," Maria stated.

Julia rolled her eyes in exasperation. "Look who's talking! Would you just look at the map and tell me where I turn right?"

"You don't. But you should have turned left at the intersection we just passed."

"Great." Julia pulled her white Ford into a shopping mall's parking lot and turned around. "How far are we from the college campus?"

"Only about five miles, I think."

"Then we won't be late. We'll probably even get there before Larry and Karl do."

"That's not saying much, considering Larry's sense of direction."

To their mutual surprise Larry and Karl were actually waiting for them in the parking lot as they arrived.

"Glad to see you made it," Larry said. "I apparently made a mistake in the directions I gave you, but I see that you coped fine."

"Julia always copes," Karl said. "Don't you know that?"

"We really should get going," Maria stated. "We've still got to find the auditorium, and we don't want to be late."

"No, we don't want to be late," Julia agreed. Though earlier she had felt uneasy about attending Adam's seminar, now she felt more relaxed, thanks to the presence of her co-workers. They'd all been working together for several months now, preparing for the Intercorp account as well as working on other projects together. She knew where she stood with Maria, Larry and Karl. And although Adam's seminar was unknown territory, at least she wasn't facing it alone. Besides, Karl was right. She *was* always able to cope.

"You know, I haven't been on a college campus in ages," Maria noted as they walked toward a group of ivy-covered brick buildings. "Not since I graduated, in fact."

"Which was what?" Larry teased her. "All of five years ago?"

At twenty-five, Maria was the baby in the group. Although Julia had to admit that sometimes she felt ten years older than the exuberant Maria, there was actually only four years' difference in their age. But thinking about age only reminded Julia that she was rapidly approaching the big three-oh, her thirtieth birthday. It was only six months away now. She hoped the upcoming seminar with Adam wouldn't age her prematurely.

Come on, she reprimanded herself. Think positively. This isn't like you. How bad can a two-hour seminar be, for heaven's sake?

Pretty bad, she soon found out. She tried; she really did try to keep an open mind. And for the first ten minutes or so she was successful. Adam's opening comments were attention grabbing but not ludicrous. Once again he had the audience in the palm of his hand.

On his own turf today, Adam was much more casually dressed than he had been at the office yesterday. He wore pleated slacks and a baggy bicycle-print shirt. More than just trendy, he also looked comfortable and very sure of himself as he moved around the lectern, eventually moving it aside entirely for more freedom of movement. He used the space between himself and the audience the way an actor uses the stage, filling it with his presence.

Julia had her notebook open and was hurriedly taking notes on the various misconceptions regarding creativity as he covered them. She was just starting to settle back and enjoy herself when . . . zap! Out of nowhere Adam came up with one of those wild antics he was so famous for.

"Okay, now that I've told you about all the myths concerning creativity, I want to show you some of the inhibitors of creativity. We all build walls around ourselves, barriers to keep everyone else out. But those barriers can also keep creativity out. Let me use an example. We've all been to a party where you start up a casual conversation without anything actually being said. You could have been talking for half an hour, and you still don't know a thing about the other person. Because of walls. People use questions as a way of diverting attention from themselves. It's the old 'Nice party, isn't it?' routine. Now I've got a little exercise that will demonstrate what I'm talking about. I want everyone to turn to the person next to you. If that person's a friend, then find someone else. Your partner should be someone you don't know. I'll need a volunteer to be my partner. How about you, in the gray business suit?''

Julia looked around.

"He's pointing at you," Maria said, nudging her.

"No, he's not." Not if he knows what's good for him, she thought to herself.

"Yes, he is," Maria insisted.

"That's right," Adam confirmed. "Come on down."

"What is this, a game show?" Julia muttered under her breath as she reluctantly got up and walked down the aisle to the front of the auditorium.

Stay calm, she told herself. You've faced crowds twice this size and done fine. You're not afraid of public speaking. Whatever it is, you can handle it. This is just one seminar out of hundreds you've given or attended. It's work. Nothing personal.

"Let's have a hand for the lovely lady who's volunteered to be my partner."

Volunteered? she thought to herself. Hardly.

"Now I want you all to speak to your partner for three minutes without asking any questions. Your comments can only be statements, personal statements about yourself, and each one has to begin with the word *I* or *My*. Remember, no questions. Just statements. One person begins and the other responds. Back and forth. Any questions? Okay then begin—'' he looked at his watch "—now."

Adam gestured for Julia to go first.

"I think this is an . . . unusual exercise," Julia stated.

"I like unusual," he replied.

"I don't."

"I know."

"Is that why you called me down here?"

"No questions," he reprimanded her. "Just comments."

You don't want to hear my comments, she thought.

Silence. Dead space. He'd talked about dead space earlier in his presentation, and how people hated it, would do almost anything to avoid it, even make the most banal of comments. She found herself guilty of the same thing.

"Nice day."

"Personal comments only," he reminded her. "Beginning with I."

"I have never attended a seminar like this before." And I hope I never have to again, a little voice inside her head added.

"I am thirty-five," he said, and then paused clearly waiting to hear her state her age.

"I am not." She was rather pleased with the way she'd sidestepped that one.

"I was born in Ventura, California."

"I wasn't."

"My family moved here to Chicago when I was seven."

"Mine didn't."

"I can see you're being difficult."

And I can see you're taking advantage of the situation, she wanted to tell him—but didn't. What harm could it do to tell him where she'd been born? None. It just felt strange; that was all. The people she'd worked with for four years didn't even know where she'd been born.

She sighed. "I was born in Germany. On an American army base near Frankfurt."

"I was in the army once."

"I find that hard to believe."

"I only lasted two weeks. I didn't follow orders very well."

"I *can* believe that."

"I enjoy teaching."

"I do, too."

His smile gave her the definite impression that he was laughing at her. She wasn't deliberately trying to be difficult; she just found it hard to share personal information with a stranger. And they didn't come much stranger than Adam.

She tried to find some sort of neutral ground. "I drive a Ford."

"I don't," he said.

She tried again. "I like to travel."

"I do, too."

Julia looked at her watch and wondered if the three minutes were up yet.

"I am not married," Adam suddenly announced, surprising her yet again.

The glint in his blue eyes told her that he expected her to avoid the topic or change the subject. Refusing to avoid the challenge, Julia said, "I'm not married, either."

To Julia's surprise, instead of following that course of questioning—or commenting, as the case was—Adam abruptly veered off into another direction. "I have four sisters."

"I have a half sister," she admitted.

"My sisters all live here in Chicago."

"My sister lives in Boston."

Adam abruptly changed subjects yet again. "My favorite movie is *Star Wars*."

"My favorite movie is *Casablanca*."

"I like pizza with everything but anchovies."

"I like deep-dish pizza with broccoli."

Adam amended his earlier statement. "I like pizza with everything but anchovies and broccoli."

"I am running out of things to say."

"I'm not," he replied with a smug grin.

"I don't have the same experience with these exercises that you have."

Adam nodded. "I probably am more experienced, that's true."

Something about the way he said the word *experienced* gave Julia the clear impression that he was referring to more than just teaching experience. She ignored the glint in his blue eyes and told herself it wasn't worth getting upset about. She refused to take the bait he was obviously giving her.

"I am sure we are both equally experienced in our own specialities," she returned calmly.

"I am looking forward to learning more about your personal specialties, but unfortunately our time is up."

"I'll go back to my seat then."

"No, wait. I'll need your help again in a few minutes. Just take a seat there in the front row, okay?"

"Okay." There, she congratulated herself as she sat down. You lived through that. It had been a bit awkward to be sure, but not too bad.

"What are some of the things you observed from that exercise?" Adam asked the group at large.

Someone raised his hand and admitted, "It was difficult."

"That's because you were breaking patterns and trying something different. Didn't you learn a lot more about your partner in those three minutes than you would have if you'd been following polite conversational patterns?"

Most people agreed.

"But some people feel uncomfortable having their walls bridged," Adam said. "And those people tend to hold a conversation like this—one person says I'm an Aquarius, and the other says I'm not. Any of you run into that or were guilty of doing that?"

Several people laughed self-consciously.

Julia tried not to squirm in her seat.

"Here's another way of breaking down those barriers I was referring to earlier," Adam continued. "For this exer-

cise I need to break the audience into three groups." He
went on to create three groups based on the beginning letter
of each person's last name. "Now I want everyone in Group
One, those with a last name beginning with *A* through *G*, to
moo like a cow. Not right this second," he added as a few
overeager seminar attendees began mooing. "In a minute or
two. Everyone in Group Two will crow like a rooster, and
everyone in the last group will meow like a cat. But wait.
There's one more thing. I want you to look at the partner
you had for the last conversational exercise. Look him or
her in the eye while you're making your animal noises. No
looking away—try not to even blink." This latest addition
to the exercise brought a great deal of good-natured groan-
ing from the audience. "It's only for sixty seconds, guys.
You can do it. Really, it's a great icebreaker."

"Okay." Adam walked over to the front row to join Julia. "Begin."

The college auditorium sounded like a barnyard. Julia did
not add her cat's meow to the many already filling the air.
She had no intention of participating in this exercise—it was
the stupidest request she'd ever heard of. Let Adam sit next
to her and make rooster noises if he wanted to. She drew the
line at that. She wouldn't even look at him, although she
had to admit he fit the part; he was as cocky as a rooster.

To Julia, the sixty seconds felt like sixty hours. Finally it
was over.

"Shame on those of you who were too uptight to join in
the fun." In front of everyone he shook a chastising finger
practically under Julia's nose. "You have to learn to loosen
your self-restraint, or you'll be too uptight for creativity to
survive. You'll choke it."

Julia knew who she wanted to choke—the rooster standing right in front of her! This was no way to run a seminar.
Not only was it humiliating, it was nonconstructive and to-
tally self-indulgent on Adam's part. The man obviously got
a kick out of standing in front of a roomful of people and

playing a high-jinx game of Simon Says, with everyone doing whatever wild antic he came up with, simply because he told them to do it.

She could feel her face getting redder by the minute. Blushing had been a curse since she'd turned twelve. She'd been able to face hostile businessmen and convince them of the advantages of updating their methods of management without flinching. But one renegade problem-solver had just managed to bring back a problem she'd thought she'd overcome years ago. She was blushing, damn it, and there was nothing she could do about it.

Adam belatedly realized he'd made a major blunder. He'd upset her. He hadn't meant to. He'd expected her to make some bantering comment intended to put him in his place. Instead her brown eyes had flashed with anger before freezing over. Learning from his mistake, for the remainder of the seminar Adam no longer spotlighted Julia's participation or lack thereof.

Afterward he intended to approach her and apologize or at least explain, but he was surrounded by students asking questions and by the time they'd dispersed, Julia had disappeared. Still there was always tomorrow. He had a meeting with the other instructors on the Intercorp project. He'd talk to Julia then.

Adam soon found out it wasn't that easy. Julia was an expert at avoiding confrontations. She was also an expert at avoiding him, not an easy thing to do when there were only the six of them in one room. But she managed it. If he was talking to Larry, she was talking to Karl. When they joined in a group discussion of the project, she spoke to the group at large and pointedly avoided looking in his direction. She was subtle, as always. Yet a whisper had always had the ability to capture his attention faster than any shout.

It took him a while, but then he could be patient when the occasion warranted it. This one did. He waited until the meeting was over and then made his move. He reached her before she could make her exit.

He put his hand on her arm, touching her with a gentleness that surprised her.

"I need to speak to you for a moment," he said.

She took a step away, dislodging his hand and thereby removing herself from his sphere of influence. "I'm giving a class in a few minutes."

"This won't take long."

"This really isn't a good time for me now. Can't we discuss whatever it is later?"

"No."

Aware of the curious looks she was getting from her colleagues, Julia relented with a nod. "All right."

"I owe you an apology," Adam said, as soon as they were alone.

"Yes, you do," she agreed quietly.

Here it was again, her unruffled composure. Instead of flaring up at him, she just stood there and looked at him, making him feel guilty all over again. But she also intrigued him.

"I shouldn't have teased you the way I did yesterday," he admitted and then felt compelled to justify his actions. "I didn't realize it would upset you that much. You've given numerous seminars yourself and are used to public speaking, to being in front of a crowd."

"I'm used to and enjoy public *speaking*," she retorted. "Not public meowing, mooing or crowing."

"That's understandable, I suppose."

She thought he looked doubtful. "You suppose?"

"You haven't done much meowing, mooing or crowing. If you had, you might feel differently about it."

"I failed to see the point of the entire exercise," she informed him coolly.

"I know you did. As I said, it's a barrier breaker."

"So's a battering ram," Julia retorted. "But that doesn't mean it's a very efficient means of communication."

She could see his smile begin in his eyes before it reached his lips.

"You may have a point there," he conceded.

"A point is much better than a battering ram."

"Ah, but some jobs require a battering ram. Nothing else will get through. A delicate little point will just go splat!"

"I can assure you that in most cases a point works much better than a battering ram. And if it doesn't work, then at least the point has gone splat and not the participant."

"You're saying I came on a little strong?"

"I'm saying that we're part of a team now, and that means working together, complementing each other's weaknesses with our strengths. It's best that you know now that my strengths do not include public displays of silliness. Yours do, and that's fine. For you. Not for me. So let's just agree to live and let live, and then maybe we'll be able to get along for the next seven weeks without too much difficulty." She held out her hand. "Agreed?"

"As I told you yesterday, I'm not very good at obeying rules."

"You're a problem-solver, right? The way to solve this problem is to do as I suggested."

"Live and let live, huh? Okay." He put his hand in hers. "I'll give it a try."

As Julia shook his hand, she felt the tingle down to her toes again and accepted it's presence with glum resignation. For a problem-solver Adam sure had a way of creating more problems than he solved!

Three

———

"Come on in and take a seat. Tomorrow is the big day. Are you ready for it?" Helen asked as Julia entered her office late Monday afternoon.

"I'm ready," Julia replied before sitting down.

"Good. Any last-minute questions before you set off for Minneapolis tomorrow afternoon?"

"None that I can think of."

"How does the team seem to be working with Adam? Any problems there?" Helen prompted.

"What makes you think there might be any problems?"

She smiled. "Julia, I've known you for four years now. I was the one who recommended you for this project, remember? I recommended you because you're the best. So is Adam. But you two are very different in your teaching approaches."

"That's certainly true. We are *very* different. In fact, I have to admit that the news of his joining us on this project took me by surprise. You'd never even hinted that you were thinking of hiring an outside consultant."

"I didn't want to say anything until the negotiations had been completed. I told you it would be a pleasant surprise," Helen reminded her. "And we really are very lucky to have gotten Adam, you know. His style may be different, but it's brilliant. Even so, I figured that you and the others would probably need a period of adjustment in order to integrate Adam into the team. That's why I've had Adam observing your sessions these past few days. How do you think that's going?"

"Fine."

"Did Adam sit in on your seminar this morning?"

Julia nodded. To her surprise, Adam had been on his best behavior and hadn't done anything to disrupt her presentation. In fact, he'd given her some very positive feedback afterward. Apparently her talk with him the other day had worked, and so far their new "live and let live" policy had been successful.

"I think it's helped Adam to see how each of us works." Julia said when Helen looked at her expectantly. "It gives him a reference point and hopefully some idea of where we're coming from."

"You know, you never did tell me what you thought of Adam's seminar."

Julia shrugged. "As you said, our presentations and our teaching methods are very different."

"Do you think that will be a problem?"

"No. Adam and I have reached an understanding."

"I'm glad to hear that. Because, as you know, this project is very important for us here at Dynamics. It's crucial that everything go smoothly. I'll want biweekly reports on your progress."

"A report for each regional office, right?"

Helen nodded. "Now as the in-house instructor with the most seniority, it will be your responsibility to make sure

that everyone else completes their reports and gets them in
to me on time. I may be the official project leader, but since
I won't actually be out on the road, you'll have to be my ears
and eyes. Keep me informed about possible trouble areas,
or negative participant response. Since Intercorp is our
largest client, the decision was made to keep an executive VP
in charge, and I was elected. Intercorp's regional managers
have been told to contact me with any questions or concerns they might have. So you see, even though I'll be here
in the office, I will still be very much involved with the im-
plementation of this project. It may mean extra work for
you, but I want you to know that if you do a good job on
this assignment, there's every indication that a position of
project leader could be yours in the future. It all depends on
you."

"I'll do my best."

"I know you will. It's just that I'm going to be depending on you twenty-four hours a day. As you know, with all
the traveling involved, this is not going to be a nine-to-five
assignment."

Julia nodded. "I realize that."

"Good. I've gone out on a limb, delegating so much responsibility to you, but I know you can handle it. And I
know you'll be able to handle Adam MacKenzie. You've got
a flair for dealing with people, Julia. It's just one of your
many talents. You've got the ability to go far in this business. That's one of the reasons why I've taken you under my
wing, as it were. You remind me of myself when I was
starting out. You've got the same tenacity, the same dedication. I know you won't let me down."

"I appreciate your faith in me, Helen. You won't regret
it."

After speaking to Helen, Julia was even more aware of the
importance of this project. It was a test, one she had to pass
with flying colors. A great deal was at stake.

With that thought in mind, Julia brought work home with her and stayed up late reading reports on Intercorp's managerial setup. Only when the graphs and flow charts began to blur before her tired eyes did she finally turn out the light. Even then, she dreamed about work.

After a morning spent clearing up last-minute problems from her desk, Julia joined Maria and Karl for a limo ride from the office to Chicago's O'Hare airport.

"Where's Larry?" Julia asked as the limo pulled out into traffic.

"He decided to ride in with his wife," Karl replied. "Said he'd meet us at the gate, the same way Adam will."

But later, as they all sat around the departure lounge, Julia started worrying. Larry was already there, talking to his wife in the corner, but there was no sign of Adam. He was certainly cutting it close, Julia noted with a frown. They were going to begin boarding the plane soon.

"What do you think happened to Adam?" she asked Maria. "He should have been here by now. He had a copy of the itinerary and knew what time our flight leaves, right?"

Maria nodded. "As far as I know, he did. I'm sure he'll be here soon. He must have gotten caught in traffic."

Just then Julia happened to look down the corridor and see that Adam had indeed gotten caught—in the arms of a beautiful stewardess!

"Ah, there's our man now," Karl noted with envious admiration. "I must say he's got good taste in women."

"That's no reason for him to be late," Julia retorted.

"Hey, with a babe like that I'm surprised he got here at all!" Karl replied.

"At least he's here now," Maria said. "We don't have to worry any more."

"Who was worried?" Julia countered. "Come on, they're boarding our row."

"Something wrong?" Maria inquired once she and Julia were both settled in their seats on the plane.

"No. Why do you ask?"

"You seemed a little uptight."

"This project is very important to me," Julia replied. "I just don't want anything going wrong."

"Nothing's going to go wrong," Maria assured her.

"I hope not."

"Excuse me, ladies, I believe I have the window seat," Adam announced as he stood in the aisle.

Maria got up but before Julia could do the same, Adam motioned her back into her seat. "Don't bother getting up. I can get past you, no problem."

Only it was a problem, of course. Even though Julia scrunched her legs all the way under the seat and as far out of the way as possible, Adam still managed to brush against her. The hum of excitement that followed the brief encounter was becoming familiar to Julia. It happened each time she and Adam came in physical contact, no matter how brief or how casual that contact might be.

He had his face turned away from her, but she caught the hint of a smile on the edge of his mouth. She also saw that he was wearing his hula-dancers tie again.

She gave a sigh of relief as he finally sat in his seat, but that relief was short-lived. When he reached for his seat belt at the same time she reached for hers, their hands collided, and more electricity was generated.

Julia looked at Adam, expecting to see a naughty glint in his eyes. Instead he looked surprisingly serious and as non-plussed as she felt. They sat there a moment, just staring at each other—hands touching—until they were interrupted by the stewardess, who was trying to get Adam's attention.

As if she'd been burned, Julia snatched her fingers away from his. Turning to face the stewardess, she realized it was the same woman he'd been embracing earlier. She was beautiful, her long black hair and almond-shaped dark eyes proclaiming her Oriental heritage. And she'd said Adam's name in the manner of someone who knew him *very* well.

But before the stewardess could say anything else, she was called away by another member of the cabin crew who needed her assistance. "I'll be back later," she promised Adam.

Karl, who along with Larry had been assigned a seat near the back of the aircraft, walked by with a huge grin and a thumbs-up sign for Adam.

Adam gave him a blank look. He then turned to Julia. "What was that all about?"

She shrugged. "I presume it was Karl's way of saying that he approves of your choice of women."

"What woman is he referring to? You?"

"Certainly not! He was referring to that stewardess of yours."

"May Ling?"

"If that's her name, then yes. What are you laughing at?"

"You'll see."

"Forget it. It's nothing to do with me." Julia reached down to get some folders out of her briefcase. She also brought out a pair of reading glasses, which she slipped on as if donning armor.

To her surprise, Adam reached into his jacket pocket and retrieved a pair of reading glasses of his own. Catching her gaze on him, he said, "Hey, small world, right? Here's just one more thing that you and I have in common."

"Which makes it about three things we have in common to a million we don't."

"Actually it's ten things to two million, but hey, who's counting? But wait, what's that I see? A smile? I believe it is. No, no good trying to hide it now, I definitely saw your lips curving up. And I must say, it looked very nice."

Her smile came out of hiding. "You're impossible."

"So I've been told. It's a requirement in my line of work."

"What line of work is that? Seducing stewardesses?"

Adam laughed again and shook his head. "If I didn't know better, I'd say you sounded almost jealous."

"You're confusing disapproval with jealousy," she returned calmly.

"You disapprove of me seducing beautiful stewardesses?"

"Only when you do it on company time, or when it makes you late for a flight."

"Otherwise it's okay?"

"You don't need my permission."

"Live and let live, hmm?"

"That's right."

"I'm afraid you've misread the situation in this particular case."

"What's that supposed to mean?"

"It means May Ling is my sister. I told you I had four of them, remember? May Ling is the youngest."

He sat back and grinned so smugly she wanted to sock him.

"She's your sister?" Maria repeated in amazement, belatedly reminding both Julia and Adam of her presence.

"There isn't much of a family resemblance, I admit," Adam said. "May Ling is Korean. My parents adopted her when she was a baby, the same way they adopted Lottie— Carlotta, when she was a baby. They flew down to Costa Rica to pick her up. I remember being quite upset that I had to stay home with my two older sisters and couldn't go along. Lottie's studying medicine now."

"And your older sisters?" Maria asked.

"They're both married and trying to raise three kids apiece. That keeps them pretty busy."

"I imagine it does," Julia noted.

"You like kids?" Adam asked her.

"I haven't had much experience with them."

"That's too bad. I really have a lot of fun with all my nephews and nieces."

"That's because he can give the kids back to our sisters when he doesn't want to play with them anymore," May Ling inserted.

"Hey," he said. "I *always* want to play."

"That's true," May Ling admitted. "He's a bigger kid than they are."

"Thanks."

"You're welcome, big brother. Can I get you something to drink before we take off?"

"No, thanks. But I would like you to meet some friendly colleagues of mine."

"Good luck working with this crazy brother of mine," May Ling said, once the introductions were made. "The stories I could tell you . . ."

"But you won't," Adam interrupted her.

"Later," May Ling promised them with a conspiratorial grin before returning to her duties.

Julia smiled and nodded her approval. "I like your sister."

"I thought you would."

Julia pondered on Adam's words long after he'd closed his eyes and gone to sleep. He'd thought about her in terms of his family and whether or not she'd like them. What did that mean? Nothing. It didn't signify anything, she told herself. It had probably just been a polite comment, a throwaway statement.

The plane dipped and swayed, returning Julia's thoughts to her immediate surroundings.

"Looks like we're hitting some rough weather," Maria said with a grimace.

The captain's announcement over the intercom system confirmed Maria's words and reminded everyone to keep their seat belts fastened. Adam kept right on sleeping.

After fastening her own seat belt, Julia tried to casually look over Adam's shoulder to make sure that his seat belt was still done up. It was. Then she decided that since she was so close to the window, she might as well lean just a little closer to get a firsthand view of how bad the weather was. As luck would have it, at that moment the plane hit another spot of turbulence, and Julia ended up sprawled against Adam's chest.

Adam's eyes flew open, and he smiled at her sleepily. "Throwing yourself at me, Julia?"

"Only in your dreams."

"How did you know?"

She frowned in confusion. "Know what?"

"About my dreams and your place in them."

"I was kidding."

"Oh, is that what you call it?"

"Why, what would you call it?"

"Flirting."

Julia's mouth dropped open. "Me? Flirt? Don't be ridiculous. I'm not the flirting type."

"I wouldn't have thought that you were the type to throw yourself into my arms either, but voilà ... here you are."

She hastily released herself. "That was an accident!"

"You don't have to get defensive. I liked having you in my arms."

"I don't find this amusing."

"Amusing's not exactly the way I'd describe it, either," he agreed. "I'd say it was more exciting, stimulating and enjoyable!"

"What are you two whispering about over there?" Maria asked.

"Semantics," Adam replied with a meaningful look in Julia's direction.

"I hate flying in bumpy weather," Maria announced nervously.

"Me too," Julia agreed and turned to engage Maria in a conversation intended to keep Maria's mind off the weather. It was not that easy keeping her own mind off Adam and his provocative comments. She didn't relish having to exchange teasing sexual banter with him for the next six weeks. They were working together, for heaven's sake! This was business. And while she had to admit that some people did mix business and pleasure, she never had.

Actually it had never become an issue before. The men she worked with—and she'd worked with quite a few—all saw her as a competent colleague, not a potential sexual partner. That hadn't happened accidentally; she'd deliberately cultivated her businesslike image. So why then wasn't that image working on Adam? Why was he ignoring her determination to keep things between them on a purely professional footing? She must be doing something wrong, but for the life of her she couldn't figure out what it was.

The thought remained in the back of Julia's mind as she gave her workshops in Minneapolis and continued to niggle at her concentration as she worked in her hotel room every night, preparing the progress reports for Helen back in Chicago. There wasn't actually enough time to stop and contemplate anything other than work, but the fleeting thoughts of Adam continued to plague her throughout the days and nights that followed, trailing her from Minneapolis to Kansas City and then to St. Louis.

It was in St. Louis that Adam decided to change the workday routine.

They'd just returned to the hotel from a hectic day spent at Intercorp's local office when Adam turned to address the group. "Do you realize that for the past twelve days we've done nothing but go from the airport, to an Intercorp office, to a hotel and then on to another airport to do the same thing all over again?"

"That's right. It's called work," Julia retorted.

"It's called dull. We need a change of scenery. What do you think, folks?"

"Sounds good to me," Karl replied.

"Me, too," Larry agreed.

"Count me in," Maria said.

"Well, what about you, Julia?" Adam prompted.

Everyone looked at her expectantly. "What kind of change of scenery are you talking about here?" she asked Adam.

Her caution made him smile. "Nothing too outrageous. Something right here in St. Louis. Only a few blocks away, as a matter of fact. What do you say?"

Not wanting to be conspicuous by her absence, Julia said, "All right. I suppose a change of scene might not be a bad idea."

"Great. We'll all go change out of these work clothes into something a little more casual and then regroup back here in the lobby in, say..." He looked at his watch. "Ten minutes. Be sure to wear comfortable shoes," he added.

With that kind of time frame to work with, everyone dispersed quickly. Julia kicked off her heels the second she entered her hotel room.

"Comfortable shoes? Casual clothes? Ten minutes? Easier said than done," she muttered as she dug in her suitcase. She hadn't exactly packed for a leisure trip. The few casual things she had brought, a sweat suit and a caftan, were hardly suitable for public attire. They were meant to be worn in the privacy of her room. She did have a comfortable pair of shoes, though. Somewhere... "Ah, gotcha!" She triumphantly tugged the pair of deck shoes out of her bag.

Ten minutes later, wearing a pair of navy pants and a silk blouse, Julia returned to their rendezvous point in the lobby.

"That's casual?" Adam inquired with a questioning lift of one eyebrow.

"It's as casual as I get on a business trip," she returned.

"I can understand that. This is as casual as I get on a business trip, too." Adam was wearing a pair of jeans and a Hawaiian-print shirt in turquoise and hot pink. He held a lightweight white linen sport jacket hooked in one finger over his shoulder. And on his feet were the strangest looking shoes. . . .

Noticing the attention she was giving his brightly colored high-top Reeboks, he lifted one foot and held it out proudly. "Nice, huh?"

"They're . . . different."

"Not really. Most of my students are wearing these."

"That explains it then. I'm not up on the current fashion trends on America's college campuses."

"You always manage to look very nice despite that drawback."

Very nice? She almost wrinkled her nose. Talk about damning with faint praise. She looked down at her outfit and suddenly wished she'd brought a pair of jeans along with her—those stretch jeans that looked really good. . . .

Wait a minute! she warned herself. Think about this. You're actually wishing that you could change the way you look just to please Adam. It might seem like a little thing, but she knew from past experience that from such little things very large problems grew.

"I like the way I look," she heard herself saying, more for her own benefit than for Adam's.

"I like the way you look, too," he agreed with one of those rakish smiles of his.

The arrival of the others prevented further discussion of Julia's appearance, much to her relief.

"So where are we going?" Karl asked after they'd walked a block or two.

"To Union Station," Adam replied.

"Why?" Julia frowned. "Are you planning on taking a train?" She wouldn't put it past him.

"It isn't a train station any longer. Now it's a National Historic Landmark and a major sight-seeing attraction with restaurants and specialty shops under the largest train-shed roof in the world."

"How do you know all that?"

"I read it in the visitor's guide in our hotel room. Didn't you read yours?"

She shook her head. "I was too busy."

"I figured you would be. Here we are." He held the door open for her.

The courteous gesture surprised her. She hadn't thought he'd be the kind for old-world manners. "Thanks."

"Yeah, thanks," said Larry, and then Maria, and then Karl as they too allowed Adam to play doorman.

To Julia's surprise Union Station was not some stuffy historical landmark, but a thriving marketplace filled with all kinds of inviting stores and restaurants. Although it was just a little before six, the place was quite crowded.

"Do you want to look around or eat first?" Adam asked.

The consensus was to look around first.

Somehow Julia and Adam ended up being paired off, with Karl, Maria, and Larry staying up ahead of them. Julia wondered if Adam had planned it that way. Then she wondered about that beautiful Waterford vase in the Irish gift shop they were passing. She stopped to look in the store's window. She loved Waterford crystal. Unfortunately this particular one was outside her budget. Sighing, Julia turned around and almost bumped into the legs of a twelve-foot stilt-walking clown!

"Careful," Adam said as she jerked back in surprise. He put a protective arm around her shoulders. "It's just one of those strolling entertainers they have going through the crowds."

"I wasn't expecting to see him there, that's all." She also hadn't expected the warm and sheltered feelings being generated by having Adam's arm around her. "Most of the shopping centers I go to don't have stilt-walking clowns."

"See what you've been missing?"

She saw in more ways than one exactly what she'd been missing. The easy comraderie, the shared smiles, the feeling of *belonging* that made her want things she shouldn't or couldn't have. She knew better. So she stepped away from Adam, but couldn't quite distance herself. Their surroundings were too frivolous for serious restraint.

An hour later they stopped for dinner at an all-you-can-eat pasta bar that served dishes from various Italian provinces. Then it was off to do more window-shopping and just plain exploring. All five of them walked around trading bags of freshly made fudge, enjoying the various sights, sounds and smells of the marketplace. Julia bought only one thing, a T-shirt that said Sure God created Man before Woman, but then you always make a rough draft before the Final Masterpiece. Maria bought one, too, and Larry got one for his wife.

Happy with their purchases, they decided to stop for drinks. Adam selected the location—the Omni Hotel's main lobby, which was located in the restored Grand Hall of the station.

As usual, his choice was excellent, Julia decided as she looked around. The six-story-high ceiling, the elaborate use of gold leaf, the stained-glass windows, everything spoke of a time when craftsmanship was still a way of life. It also created a romantic ambience that lowered her defenses.

And so it was that as they sat around, enjoying their drinks and sharing conversation, Julia found herself joining in on a more personal level than usual.

"My wife would love it here," Larry said. "So would my daughter for that matter."

"You miss them, don't you?" The observation came from Adam.

Larry nodded. "We've only been away less than two weeks, but at times it seems longer than that."

"I know what you mean," Julia murmured.

Everyone looked at her in surprise.

"*You're* homesick?" Larry asked in disbelief.

"I didn't say that. I only said that it seems like we've been away longer than two weeks."

Larry nodded. "I didn't think you could be homesick. Not you."

"Why not me?" she said defensively.

"Because whenever we're out of town on business you seem to thrive on the traveling."

"Maybe I'm just getting older."

"That's right." Larry grinned. "You *are* going to hit thirty this year, aren't you?"

"Not until January."

"I had a great time on my thirtieth birthday," Adam inserted.

"That figures," she muttered.

"Are you upset about this landmark occasion?" Adam asked.

"Not really."

"Which means yes," he translated.

"Which means maybe," she corrected him.

"What do you usually do for your birthday?"

"Ignore it and hope it will go away."

"Well, that's the problem right there then. Haven't you heard that you're supposed to enjoy birthdays? Have a party, sing *Happy Birthday*, open presents, eat birthday cake—the whole enchilada."

"Birthday cakes and enchiladas don't appeal to me," she retorted.

"Okay, then how about a hot-fudge sundae instead of cake and Tchaikovsky's 1812 Overture instead of *Happy Birthday*?"

She was touched that Adam had remembered her saying that she liked sundaes and Tchaikovsky.

He smiled and nudged her with his knee. "See that doesn't sound so bad, does it?"

She had to admit, even if just to herself, that it didn't sound bad at all. In fact, it sounded downright appealing. Just the way Adam could be downright appealing. It had not escaped her notice that an attraction was growing between them. She didn't know what else to call this awareness, this higher level of sensitivity whenever he was near. Attraction seemed like a good word for it.

Taking another sip of her Drambuie, she wondered if the after-dinner drink was responsible for dulling the sharp edges of her concern. It seemed like too much trouble to worry about things tonight. So she just sat back and enjoyed.

When they did get up to leave, she said, "This was a good idea."

"Thanks," Adam replied. "It was between this and the National Bowling Hall of Fame."

"You made the right choice," she assured him with a smile.

"Wait, before we leave, there's one more thing I want to show you." He led her down the steps to the station's front entryway. "Here, stand right here." He faced her toward the wall.

"What are you doing, Adam?" Karl asked. "Putting Julia in the corner for misbehaving in class?"

"Very funny," Julia retorted.

"Come on, guys." Maria took Larry and Karl by the arm. "Time to leave."

"Wait!" Julia called out. "Where are you going?"

"Larry's going to call home while Karl and I go get another bag of that delicious fudge," Maria answered. "We'll be back shortly."

Before Julia knew what had happened, she and Adam were alone. She shifted nervously. "What are you up to?"

"Nothing illegal. Just stay there a minute," Adam told her as he walked to the other side of the entryway.

A second later she heard her name being spoken in a sexy whisper that actually made her shiver. She looked around in confusion, trying to figure out where the sound had come from.

"Right here, Julia," she heard a man say, still softly, and still sexily. "It's a whisper arch. Try it."

"Adam?"

"That's right."

"I feel strange talking to a wall."

"You're talking to me, not to the wall. And I have to say that you have a very sexy whisper, Julia. It makes me want to do things you wouldn't approve of."

"What kind of things?" she asked and then could have bitten her tongue for doing so.

He laughed softly. "Nothing too outrageous. Just kissing you. That wouldn't be so bad, would it?"

"Yes, it would."

"What was that? I couldn't hear you."

"You heard me just fine," she retorted.

"You said yes, right?"

"No. I mean, yes."

"Doesn't sound to me like you know what you mean."

"You're confusing me."

"That's a start."

"And this is the end. This ridiculous conversation is now over. Do you hear me?"

"I hear you," Adam said from right behind her. "But who are you talking to?"

Startled, she turned around. "You. What are you doing here? I thought you were over there on the other side of the archway."

"That's what you thought, huh?"

"Come on, Adam, you're not going to try and pretend that you weren't just on the other side of this whispering arch."

"Is that what this is? A whispering arch? I wondered why you were talking to the wall."

"Keep that act up and people will be wondering why you've got a black eye," she warned him.

"All right." He teasingly held up his hands in a gesture of surrender. He gave her an approving nod before adding, "So you do have a temper after all."

Her anger increased. "Is that what that little exercise was all about, to see if I have a temper? Is this your way of doing a little course work on the side, pressing buttons and seeing what happens?"

"Julia, I'd never dream of pressing your buttons or anything else for that matter without an invitation."

His teasing comment only infuriated her further. "This is all just a game to you, isn't it? A test."

He frowned. "Why are you getting so upset?"

"Because I don't appreciate being used as a human guinea pig in one of your little barrier-breaking exercises."

"Hey, calm down. It wasn't anything like that."

"You two all right?" Maria asked as she, Larry and Karl rejoined them.

"Everything's fine," Julia stated.

"I'm bushed," Maria announced. "Are you ready to go back to the hotel now?"

Julia nodded.

"I think it's time we all headed back," Adam said.

The return trip was much quieter than the outward one had been. Believing in safety in numbers, Julia deliberately stayed right between Maria and Larry. It had been a long evening, and everyone was tired. Once back at the hotel, they all headed straight for the elevators and entered the same one. The problem was that Larry, Karl and Maria all got off on the fifteenth floor while Adam and Julia both had rooms on the sixteenth floor.

"There's something we need to clear up," Adam said as soon as the others had gotten off, leaving them alone in the elevator. "You misunderstood me earlier. I never intended to test you."

"No? Then what was your intention?"

"To kiss you. Don't scrunch against the wall like that!" He gave her a chastising look. "I didn't say I was going to kiss you right *here* or right *now*." The elevator doors opened and he gestured for her to go ahead of him. "I do have some idea of proper social behavior, you know. I realize that a gentleman doesn't kiss a lady in an elevator, at least not until he knows her better. A gentleman only kisses a lady after he's escorted her to her door. Which is right here, right? Room 1604?"

She nodded.

"Then I'll say good-night the way a gentleman would." With a grin, he leaned down to place a very chaste kiss on her forehead.

And it would have ended there had Julia not chosen that moment to lift her face. The moment she looked into his eyes she was lost.

Adam whispered her name again, just as he had earlier. Only this time he was standing so close that she could feel his breath on her lips. Her mind suddenly went blank.

Common sense disappeared as her other senses took over. She could feel her heart pounding, could hear her breath catch as his lips brushed hers. It was a soft kiss, a gentle beginning to what became a seductive exploration. His mouth was warm and so gently coaxing that she couldn't help but respond.

There wasn't time for thought; she was working on instincts. And those instincts told her to give what his lips asked for, to take what his mouth was offering. Her own lips first softened and then gradually parted.

Adam didn't immediately take advantage of her capitulation. Instead he demonstrated his creativity by brushing feather-light kisses across her mouth, until her lips tingled and she ached for something more substantial than this sensual teasing.

He soon gave it to her, deepening the kiss, slowly increasing the intimacy, the pleasure. His hands, which had been resting on her shoulders, slid down her back to pull her closer to him. She went willingly, blindly. Her body conformed to the hard angles of his as if solely designed for that very purpose. But it wasn't long before reality returned, warning her of the danger of her actions.

What was she doing? she asked herself. This couldn't continue. She was standing in front of her hotel-room door making out with a business associate. A fully aroused business associate who could kiss like an angel and seduce like the devil. It had to stop. Now!

Even so, she found it hard to break off the embrace. It took a lot of determination, but she did move away from him. Blinking myopically, Julia took one step backward, then two, until she bumped into the door at her back. All the while she was frantically trying to come up with something brilliant to say, something nonprovocative, something guaranteed to diffuse the situation. Nothing came to mind.

To her surprise Adam didn't say anything, either. It was the first time she'd ever seen him at a loss for words. When she'd finally gathered enough composure to speak, he put his fingers on her lips and shook his head.

Taking her keys from her hand, he unlocked her door, returned the keys to her and gave her just one husky suggestion. "Lock your door."

Then he was gone.

Four

____

That kiss haunted Julia all night and throughout the next day. She dreamed about it, woke up thinking about it. She wasn't even safe in her seminars. She'd be in the middle of a discussion on improving efficiency and wham, she'd remember the feel of Adam's lips on hers. She managed to cover her distraction, but its very existence disturbed her.

Professionally she couldn't afford any diversions right now—and heaven knows Adam was one extremely sexy diversion! It was very important that she do well with this assignment; Helen had made that clear to her before they'd left Chicago. Julia knew this was her big chance to finally prove herself.

But there was another even larger reason for avoiding Adam, one she was hesitant to admit even to herself. The bottom line was that she couldn't afford any romantic entanglements, and it wasn't just because of her job; it was because of her track record. Julia knew her weaknesses, knew her own strengths. She didn't do well at relation-

ships; it was as simple as that. The more she wanted them to
succeed, the more they seemed to fail.

The truth was she cared too much. She couldn't dole out
her emotions in half measures, or even in manageable measures. It was all or nothing with her. And her all was too
overwhelming. "Suffocating me with emotion" was the way
Bob, the last man in her life, had put it.

She was a woman who loved too much. There had been
books written about women like her, and she'd read them
all. They'd helped her identify her problem, but so far they
hadn't helped her cure it. But then she could hardly expect
a lifetime's worth of behavior to be changed overnight.

"It'll be okay. I'll take care of you." Julia had said it as
a five-year-old to her mother after her father had deserted
them. But it had taken another man, Tom Brinkman, to
make her mother laugh again. They'd been married twenty-
four years now, and they'd had a beautiful daughter together—Patti. A daughter who made them both very happy.
Unlike Julia....

"It'll be okay. I'll take care of you." More recently Julia
had said those words to the misunderstood and brooding
Bob when he'd been fired from his fourth job in as many
months. *"Just tell me what I can do to help."* In the end
there had been nothing she could do to help, but that hadn't
stopped her from trying. It had taken a job offer in California to help Bob. He'd left Julia without a second thought
and without inviting her along. Once again she hadn't
pleased someone she'd loved.

Ah, the need to please. It certainly *had* gotten her into
plenty of emotional hot water. Lately—for her own preser-
vation—she'd had to dam up her emotions to keep them
under control. That included temporarily swearing off all
romantic involvements.

It had worked fine so far. No one had guessed that beneath her calm exterior was a woman who went off the deep
end. Until Adam had come along.

Now he was starting to push buttons she didn't want pushed. She wondered why he was doing it—giving her those meaningful looks, those intimate smiles, the silent messages that said, *You're special.* Was it a game to him? A challenge? A minor diversion to stave off the boredom of being on the road?

Whatever it was, it couldn't go on. She had to confront Adam and put this flirtatious pursuit of his to an end. The confrontation came in Dallas the very next day.

They'd taken a cab into the city from the airport. Julia had hoped to share her cab with Maria, or even with Larry or Karl, but Adam had maneuvered it so that he rode with her, and the other three shared a cab of their own.

The cab had barely taken off from the curb when Adam tugged Julia into his arms and kissed her. Caught completely off guard, Julia responded for an instant before hastily pulling away.

She was too breathless to speak, but inside her head the recriminations were already flying. *Nice going. Why didn't you keep your cool and keep your distance?*

I was in a cab, she defended herself. *How was I supposed to know he'd kiss me? Forget it. Concentrate now on damage control.* How could she make up for the ground she'd lost, let alone the credibility?

Adam didn't seem at all upset by her retreat or her subsequent silence. "I was just making sure I didn't dream that kiss outside your room in St. Louis," he explained with a grin. "We haven't had a second alone since then."

"I know." Julia placed her briefcase on the seat between them. "I planned it that way."

Adam noted the barrier with a raised eyebrow. "Something wrong?"

"Yes."

"Are you going to tell me what it is, or am I going to have to guess?"

"I don't think a cab is the proper place for the kind of discussion I had in mind."

"Okay. Where do you want to have this discussion? Some place quiet I presume?"

She could almost hear the phrase "Your room or mine" coming up. "No." She leaned forward and closed the glass panels separating them from the cabby. "I've decided we should have our discussion right here, after all." Taking a deep breath, she got right to the point. "Look, we have to talk about that kiss the other night. And the one you just stole."

"Stole?"

She waved away his objection. "It can't happen again, Adam. No more little touches, no more looks and no more kisses."

He gave her a bland I-don't-know-what-you-mean look that infuriated her.

"You know exactly what I'm talking about," she said. "You're doing it deliberately. I don't know why you're doing it, but I want you to stop. We're colleagues working on a very important project together. That's all we are."

"Do you kiss all your colleagues the way you kissed me?"

"No, of course not!"

"Then I'd say we're more than just colleagues, wouldn't you?" he said.

"Let me put it this way. I have a golden rule of never mixing business with pleasure."

"You've never heard the saying that rules are made to be broken?"

"I've heard it. I just don't subscribe to it."

"So where does that leave us?"

"As colleagues and that's all."

"No more kisses?"

"No."

"You're afraid."

You bet I am, she thought to herself. Aloud she said, "I don't have to justify my feelings. Why are you pursuing this anyway?"

"Pursuing you, you mean?"

She nodded.

"Maybe because you're a whisper and not a shout."

"What's that supposed to mean?"

"Still waters run deep. You hide your light under a bushel, and I'm curious to know why."

Julia shifted uncomfortably. Adam was definitely getting too close for comfort here, not just physically but emotionally as well. She didn't want him trying to figure her out. So she responded with cool derision. "And I'm curious to know why you, the creativity specialist, are suddenly talking in clichés."

"You've driven me to it," he readily admitted. "See what you've done to me?"

"It was unintentional, I assure you."

"I know that, and it only makes it worse." He heaved a dramatic sigh and shook his head in mock dismay. "You haven't tried to grab my attention, but you've quietly gotten it anyway. You're an intriguing mass of contradictions."

"Well, this intriguing mass would prefer your focusing your attention elsewhere. I realize this is probably just a game to you, your way of amusing yourself while we're on the road, but I don't find it very funny."

"I'm not laughing, either," he said quietly. "You still think I'm playing games with you? I thought we cleared that up in St. Louis." He gently caressed her cheek with his hand. "I don't consider you to be a diversion, Julia. I like you. I want to get to know you better. What's so bad about that?"

She shook her head, dislodging his seductive fingers. "We're working together, Adam. Anything else would make things very complicated, and I can't cope with that right now. This project is very important to me, and its success is very important to my future.''

"And what kind of future do you see for yourself, Julia?" he asked impatiently. "Married to your job?''

"Not necessarily, no. What kind of future do you see for yourself?''

One that includes you. The thought hit Adam with the force of a sledgehammer.

"See, it's not that easy when you're the one answering the questions, is it?'' she countered.

He slid his fingers between hers. "You can feel what's happening between us. Trying to ignore it won't make it go away. It's real, and it's very strong. It's worth exploring, Julia. Think about it.''

She did think about it, from Dallas to Houston to Boston, all in the space of five days. During that time Adam was on his best behavior, no more stolen kisses. But he still gave her those looks that made her hungry for more than just visual communication. And he still managed to touch her at least a dozen times a day—casual touches, courteous touches, that all carried a deeper message of desire.

The nights were the worst. She dreamed of him—frequently and in vivid detail. The dreams were so realistic that she would wake up, convinced that he'd been there with her, touching her, teasing her, promising to satisfy her needs only to disappear before she was fulfilled. It left her feeling frustrated to put it mildly.

Her mood wasn't improved any by the work load, which seemed to double every day. In addition to the regional reports she was gathering, she also had to wade through piles of participant response forms, compiling the comments and reactions that were listed there. She was half afraid she'd find a notation saying "Seminar leader obviously had her mind on other things—a man perhaps?" but the feedback had mostly been positive, so far. The managers in the

Houston office had been somewhat resistant to some of her ideas, though, and she noted that in her final report.

Julia removed her reading glasses and rubbed the bridge of her nose. There weren't enough hours in the day. She was getting behind, and she hated the feeling. She couldn't blame it all on Adam; the problem was with her. Not only did she have her reluctant attraction to him to contend with, but here she was in Boston—home of her younger half sister, Patti—and she was feeling guilty at not having contacted her yet. She couldn't in good conscience put off phoning her any longer.

I'll make it a quick call, Julia decided. Just a few minutes of conversation. I'll keep it light and friendly. We won't argue this time. I'll tell Patti that I'm only in town for a few days and didn't have any extra time for visiting.

Of course it didn't work out that way. As soon as Patti found out Julia was in Boston she insisted on coming to get her and having a visit.

"I'm only going to be here three days," Julia stated, just as she'd practiced. "I'll be working most of the time."

"What about the evenings?" Patti demanded. "You must have the evenings free?"

"Actually the seminars often run into the evening."

"Tonight then. It's Sunday."

"I've got a lot of work to get done by tomorrow morning."

"If you don't want to see me, you can just tell me," Patti said petulantly.

Julia sighed. "That's not it."

"Good. Then Jerry and I will come pick you up at the hotel in forty minutes. We'll be driving a red BMW. See you soon."

"No, Patti, wait...."

But the line was already dead. Muttering under her breath, Julia hung up the phone. Patti always did this to her.

Always made her feel guilty. And always ended up getting her own way.

Looking into the dresser mirror, Julia's mind suddenly flashed back to their very first Christmas together. She'd been seven, and Patti had only been two months old. The image was so clear that she could almost hear her own high-pitched voice saying, "Look, Mommy, I got you the best Christmas present! I made it special just for you. Open mine next!"

Her mother hadn't even looked at her, or at the artwork Julia had so painstakingly wrapped all by herself. "Mommy already has the best Christmas present," she'd crooned, looking down at her newest daughter. "A perfect little baby girl named Patti."

Later that day Julia had found the painting she'd done for her mother in the garbage along with the other discarded Christmas wrappings. Patti had spit up all over it. A critic even then, she thought to herself with bittersweet humor. It had been a stupid little incident, but somehow it still had the power to hurt. She closed her eyes and willed the unhappy memories away.

You're all grown up now, she reminded herself. You make a living out of dealing with people, all kinds of people. Difficult ones are supposed to be your specialty. So why was it that the minute she spoke to Patti, those years of training flew out the window and she regressed back to the little girl who wanted to make everyone happy and never quite succeeded?

It was no good brooding about it. She and Patti had never had a smooth relationship. The best she could do was hope the evening wouldn't go too badly. Unfortunately things did not start out auspiciously.

"So, Julia, you're going to be thirty soon," Patti noted within four minutes of picking her up. "When are you going to get married and settle down? It's the only way to live, right, honeybun?" she said to her husband.

"Right, sugarplum."

After half an hour of this sort of saccharine sweetness, Julia lost her appetite. Two hours of questioning about her life-style, and she began losing her temper.

"Oh, you career women are all alike," Patti was saying. "You never take the time to spend with family. You know Mom and Dad haven't seen you in almost two years. And you never call Mom. She told me so."

Mom and Dad. It sounded very homey. But the problem was that Patti's dad wasn't really hers, and the subtle distinction had always made Julia feel awkward around him. But that was just one of the many things she never talked about with her family. Instead she used the old reliable excuse, "I've been busy."

"You're not the only one with a busy life, you know, Julia. I'm busy too. But I call Mom at least once a week. And Phoenix is further from Boston than it is from Chicago, so our phone bill is higher, but it's worth it, right, honeybun? My guy's so understanding." Patti patted her husband's hand. "I don't know what I'd do without him. And I don't know how you cope on your own, Julia."

"You get used to it."

"Why would you want to?"

"Because I like it."

Patti persisted. "What do you like about it?"

"The independence."

"What does that word really mean? I don't understand the concept at all."

"I know," Julia noted dryly.

"What's that supposed to mean?"

"Nothing."

"Everything you say always means something, Julia. So what did you mean this time? Are you saying that I'm not independent? You're right. And I don't want to be. But that doesn't mean I'm dependent. I prefer to think that my Jerry and I are interdependent. We both depend on each other in different ways. After all, men and women are different, and they both have different strengths and weaknesses. I can't understand why some women try so hard to be like men."

"Meaning that you think I'm trying to be like a man?"

"You don't act very femininely. The past three times I've seen you, you've always been wearing a business suit."

"And what's wrong with that? I am a businesswoman, Patti. I work for a living."

"So do I. Just because I choose to stay home and take care of my family, that doesn't mean I don't work. I work just as hard as you do, Julia."

"I'm sure you do."

"And don't be so condescending. You always think you know best."

"Listen," Julia countered heatedly, "I'm not the one who was attacking your life-style, the one who said that my way was the only way of living. If there's any attacking being done here, it's being done by you!"

"Sure, shift the blame onto me!" Patti retorted.

"Hey, you two. How about dessert?" an uncomfortable "honeybun" asked.

Julia took a deep breath before replying, "Nothing for me, thanks. I'd better be getting back to the hotel. It's getting late. But if you two want to stay, I can take a cab, no problem."

"Absolutely not. We picked you up. We'll take you back, right, honeybun?"

"Right, sugarplum."

"There's no need."

"Stop arguing, Julia."

After that Julia just quit talking, period.

The return ride was marked by tense silence, and Julia longed for the sanctuary of her hotel room. She jumped from the car with a murmured word of thanks and blindly headed for the hotel's revolving doors. She shoved at the metal handle with more force than was necessary. Her forward motion was powerful enough to send her barreling out of the revolving doors. She bumped smack into Adam.

He put his hands under her elbows to prevent her from falling. "Whoa. Where's the fire?"

When she didn't answer him, Adam looked at her eyes. She was upset. He could see that much. He could also feel her trembling in his arms, and as much as he would like to take the credit and say that his nearness had elicited this response from her, he could tell that her agitation was more negative than seductive.

"What's wrong?" he asked in such a concerned way that Julia had to blink back the tears. "Julia?"

She sniffed and bit her tongue to prevent herself from bursting into tears. This was ridiculous. She had to get herself back under control.

"It's okay." He stroked her back, comforting her. "Whatever's wrong, it'll be okay."

His touch was not only soothing, it also made her feel cared for, and that wasn't a feeling she'd experienced much.

"Come on." He nudged her forward.

"Where are we going?"

"To a little place just around the corner. It's quiet, and we can talk there. They also serve the best hot-fudge sundae in Boston, or so I'm told."

Fifteen minutes later, with spoon in hand, Julia tasted the sundae the waitress had just placed in front of her. "It *is* good."

"I'm glad. Now that you're getting your dose of chocolate, maybe you can tell me what that was all about back there in the hotel lobby. What happened?"

Julia shrugged uneasily. "The aftereffects of seeing my half sister, I guess."

"Did you two have an argument?"

"Not exactly. I don't know how to explain it. We just seem to rub each other the wrong way. I'm never able to say the right thing to her. You'd think I'd be able to. I mean that's part of my training, dealing with people and learning how to smooth out the rough edges so that people can work together more effectively.''

''But we're not talking about people here, we're talking about your family.''

''I seem to be able to get along with strangers better than I can with family.''

Adam nodded understandingly. ''A lot of people feel that way.''

''You don't.''

''There are times I do. But generally speaking I've been lucky. I'm pretty close to my family now. Of course, having them all in the immediate area helps. We're forced to get along.''

''Geographic distance doesn't have anything to do with it. It's the emotional distance. I don't have anything in common with Patti.''

''Tell me about her.''

''She's seven years younger than I am, happily married, the mother of an angelic two-year-old girl. She's the apple of my mom's eye.''

''Who is? The angelic two-year-old or Patti?''

''Both of them.''

''What about you?'' he asked.

''Me? I feel closer to the people I work with than I do to my family.''

''Meaning that they've become a surrogate family to you?''

''I guess they have.''

Adam frowned. ''That isn't necessarily a good thing.''

''Why not?''

''Because you're not leaving yourself open for any new relationships, or giving yourself time to work on old ones. By centering so much of your life around your job, you're putting all of your emotional eggs in one basket, so to speak. And it's a fragile basket at that. People change jobs, move away...."

"I didn't mean that I depend on the people I work with. I just meant that I get along with them better."

"You don't depend on anyone, do you?"

"Only myself."

"A good philosophy when taken in moderation. But 'No man is an island'."

"I'm not an island. I see people, a lot of people, every day."

"Most of those people you'll never see again after their seminar is completed. I'll admit that it's a perfect place to hide, but it's not a healthy one."

"What are you talking about? Who's hiding?"

"You are."

"From what?"

"From your emotions. By focusing all your attention on your work you don't have to think about anything else. You become immersed in it, almost obsessed by it. It becomes the center of your universe, the sole source of your identity. You soon lose track of what's happening in the real world."

"What do you, in your ivory tower at the university, know about the real world?" she retorted, irritated by his comments.

"I'm still learning about the real world, but I am an expert on the world where you reside, the business world. I know all about the fourteen-hour workdays, the seven-day workweeks, the need to get ahead and then the struggle to stay there. I haven't always worked at a college. I was in the private sector for five years. I was the youngest head of research and development in the country. That just meant I had to be better than all the rest. Always proving myself. Working longer hours, taking on extra projects, extra responsibility until..."

"Until what?"

"Until I collapsed in the office one day and woke up in the hospital. I had a ruptured appendix."

"Surely you're not blaming that on your job?"

"No. But as I was being prepped for emergency surgery I realized that life isn't an open-ended gift. Time is not unlimited, and it shouldn't be wasted, because it can't be replaced."

"So you consider the time you spend doing research as time wasted?"

"No, but it wasn't necessarily time spent prudently. Sure, I was good at my job, but I was isolated and lonely. I hadn't seen my family in months, even though they all lived nearby. I didn't have the time. I'd lost track of personal friends, again because I didn't have the time to keep in touch with them. I was like a hamster on one of those little wheels, and I was just running in circles. The faster I ran, the faster I had to run just to keep up. I made the conscious decision to get off that hamster wheel and enjoy my life by achieving some balance in it."

"Are you saying my life isn't balanced?" she demanded.

"Would you say it was?"

"I'm happy with my life the way it is."

"You didn't look very happy when you came into the hotel."

"That's because my sister was trying to tell me how to run my life, the same way you're doing right now."

"I'm just saying that I recognize what you're doing because I've been there myself. What's so bad about that?"

"What's good for you isn't automatically good for me."

"Being so obsessed with work, the way you are, isn't good for anyone. From what you said about your family, it sounds to me as if you're trying to get the approval at work that you never got from your family. Here at Dynamics you can be the apple of someone's eye, if not your mom's then your boss's."

His comment was a low blow, and it left Julia feeling painfully betrayed. She'd opened herself up to him, and this was how he repaid her—by throwing her words back in her face? "Thank you, Doctor, for that idiotic piece of amateur psychoanalysis!" she retorted angrily. "You know what your problem is?"

"No," he replied wryly, "but I'm sure you're going to tell me."

"Damn right I am. You love playing God. You like standing in front of an audience and making them do whatever you tell them to do. You like the control, the power."

"I'm just trying to help you."

"I don't need your help. And even if I did, what makes you think you're qualified enough to offer it? What makes you the expert? The fact that you're a problem-solver? If you ask me, you create more problems than you solve. You've very good at stepping back and telling other people what's wrong with their lives. It's not a very appealing characteristic. In fact your know-it-all approach is aggravating, to put it mildly. You may be an expert at problem-solving, but you're not an expert about me or my problems. You don't even know me."

"I know you better than you think, Julia. That's why you're getting angry. Because I came a little too close for comfort."

"And you're always right, is that it?" With calm control, Julia pulled her wallet from her purse, placed a five on the table and got up. "In case no one has told you this before, Adam, let me be the first to do so. Self-appointed experts are a real pain in the behind. Good night."

Five

Adam soon learned something else about Julia. She held a grudge. She might be slow to anger, but she was equally slow to forgive and forget. Not that he felt he'd done anything that needed forgiving.

Maybe he had come on a bit strong, but he was worried about her. He saw such great potential in her. Despite the image she projected, he knew she wasn't basically a distant or cold person. Beneath her calm exterior was a deep reservoir of emotion, just waiting to be tapped. All the signs were there.

There were other signs too, signs that told Adam that this was getting serious. He had only to touch her, and he was on fire. He kissed her and forgot where he was. He wanted her, and he suspected she wanted him, too. So why couldn't they just enjoy each other? Why was she creating problems?

Maybe Julia was right, he conceded. Maybe he was approaching her as a problem-solver would, looking for a way to get the end result he wanted—her in his bed. But damn it, there had to be a way of getting through to her. He just had to look at the situation from another perspective.

That however was hard to do when Julia treated him as if he were invisible.

Her coolness toward Adam did not go unnoticed by the others.

The first question came from Maria. "What's going on between you and Mad Mac?"

Julia had almost forgotten Adam's nickname. If only she could forget him half as easily. "Nothing's going on. Why do you ask?"

"Because you're ignoring him."

"Am I?"

"You know you are. The question is *why* are you doing it?"

"We had a disagreement," Julia said.

"About work?"

"No."

"Oh." Maria nodded knowingly. "I see."

"No, you don't see! I don't see either!" Julia paused a moment to regain her composure. "We argued in Boston," she finally admitted. "I'd just had a disastrous visit with my half sister, and Adam took the opportunity to tell me how I was obsessed with work and how I was just generally messing up my life."

"And you took exception to that?"

"Wouldn't you?" Julia countered.

"Yes. But I can't help wondering why Adam thought he had to give you advice."

"He just likes telling people how to live their lives."

"He hasn't tried giving me advice, except on how to improve my presentation. And he was right," Maria added thoughtfully.

Julia shook her head. "That's exactly what I mean. He's giving you advice on something that's your specialty."

"Yes, but he was right," Maria pointed out.

"Another thing I dislike about him," Julia muttered darkly.

"Why don't you tell me what's *really* going on here?"

"Oh, please, Maria. Put your psychology-major voice away."

"Hey, if you don't want to talk about it . . ."

"I'm sorry. I didn't mean to snap at you." Julia rubbed her forehead where a headache had been nagging all day. "I don't seem to have much patience lately."

"That's not surprising, considering the hours you're putting in."

"We're all putting in a lot of hours."

"But you're putting in more than the rest of us."

"I've got a lot at risk here."

"It's just a job, Julia. It's not worth getting sick over."

"Who's getting sick?"

"You don't look well."

She smiled wanly. "Gee, thanks."

"Hey, I'm just calling it as I see it."

"You need glasses."

Maria grinned. "You may be right. So how long are you going to give Adam the cold shoulder?"

"Did he send you here to talk to me?" Julia demanded.

"No, suspicious one, Adam did not send me here. I came all on my very own, to give you my regional report like a good little seminar instructor. And to satisfy my curiosity about you and Adam."

"There's nothing between Adam and myself except ill will at the moment."

"He doesn't seem to be angry at you," Maria said.

"Why should he be? *I* didn't do anything wrong."

"And he did?"

"I already told you he did."

Maria nodded. "Giving unasked-for advice is a punishable crime here in Boston, I understand."

"Can we change the subject, please?" Julia requested.

"Sure thing. What else do you want to talk about?"

"How was the feedback from your Houston sessions? Did you notice a difference in the response of the participants?"

Maria sighed. "That's shoptalk. Can't we talk about something other than work just for a few minutes? Frankly I could use the time to unwind. These past three weeks have been pretty hectic."

"Agreed."

Yet, even Maria apparently found she had little else but work on her mind. "I can't believe we're only halfway through this project. I'm glad I'm going home this weekend. For one thing, I'm sick of looking at the same six suits I brought. I'm going to completely restock my suitcase when I get home. How about you? When are you going back home?"

"I'm not sure. I've got so much work to do, it really doesn't pay for me to take the time to fly all the way back to Chicago and fly back a day later. It's not as if I have family, like Larry does."

"And it's not as if you get homesick or anything."

"Right."

Maria shook her head. "You really do like life on the road? Doesn't the impermanence, the constant movement, the change ever get to you? Don't you long to sleep in your own bed, put your head on your own pillow, wrap yourself in your own towels?"

To which Julia replied, "My mattress at home isn't as comfortable as most of the hotel beds I've slept in on the road, ditto for the towels. As for my own pillow, I brought it along with me. I always do when I travel."

"So you're perfectly happy with this way of life?"

Julia nodded. "For the most part. Sure, there are times when I look at my limited wardrobe and I want to scream. And some of the hotel's dry-cleaning service leaves a lot to be desired. I've got two blouses that may never be the same again. However, there are pluses."

"Name some."

"Room service. I like having a waiter bringing me food at the drop of a phone receiver."

"Room service isn't bad," Maria grudgingly agreed. "But those minibars have got to go. They're nothing but temptation. I'm not talking about the drinks they have in there, I'm talking about the cookies. It kills me that a little box with four Oreos in it costs more than a huge package does."

"I have to admit, that gets me too," Julia said with a grin. "I've been known to raid that minibar in the middle of the night."

Maria nodded. "Me, too. But I always feel guilty charging that onto my room costs—as if Helen is going to check my expense account and find those Oreos. She'll shake her head and say 'Inefficient cost management, Maria!'"

"I think she'd understand. Helen's got her weaknesses, too."

"I don't know about that. She's a pretty tough cookie. You have to be to have gotten to the position she's gotten to."

"She may be tough, but she's fair."

"Is it fair to have loaded you with so much extra work on this project?"

"Helen's giving me a chance to prove myself here," Julia said somewhat defensively. "And I appreciate the trust she has in me."

"Just take some advice and don't wear yourself ragged trying to get everything done," Maria warned.

"How come everyone suddenly feels the need to give me advice?" Julia asked in exasperation.

"'Cause we care about you, you lucky girl, you!"

While Julia and Maria were talking up in Julia's hotel room, Adam and Larry were down in the lobby, having a drink together. Adam tried telling himself that he wasn't really pumping Larry for information, he just wanted to have a talk with him. And if the conversation should just happen to turn to the subject of Julia, then hey, what was wrong with that? All he wanted was Larry's perspective on Julia. Adam hoped it might help him regain a little perspective of his own. It didn't take much coaxing to get Larry started.

"She really is the best efficiency consultant I've ever run across," Larry said. "I was with another management firm before joining Dynamics, and the efficiency people there were nothing compared to Julia. She's able to really translate her concepts into situations that managers can relate to. Her sessions really do lead to improved production from employees...."

Adam tuned out the rest of what Larry was saying. This was all very interesting, but he already knew that Julia was good at her job. He wanted to know more. So he tossed out a statement intended to get a reaction. "You know, people tend to think of efficiency experts as being cold and unfeeling," he commented.

"Julia doesn't conform to that stereotype at all," Larry maintained. "Oh, she may be quiet, but she's not cold. She's just self-contained. But she's always ready to help someone out, whether it's a problem at work or at home. I'd hate to tell you how many times she's sat down and listened to my problems."

"Has she ever returned the favor and consulted you with a problem of hers?"

Larry paused a moment before shaking his head. "Come to think of it, she hasn't, but then Julia tends to go it alone. She has a resiliency, an ability to cope that appears to be just about endless. She's always cool in a crisis. She gives solid advice, too, but she always waits until she's asked."

Adam shifted in his seat. "Yeah, I guess there's nothing worse than a know-it-all who gives out unasked-for advice, huh?" he noted with false bravado.

Larry nodded. "You got that right."

"So Julia gives good advice, huh?"

"She sure does. Why? Have you got a problem?"

"Who doesn't have problems?" Adam returned wryly.

"Yeah, I guess you're right. Anything you want to talk about?"

"Thanks, but no thanks." This was one problem Adam had to figure out on his own.

Julia had a problem. She was definitely not feeling well, and it was more than just fatigue. "You are not getting sick," she told herself as she got up early on Saturday morning. She would have been more reassured if her voice hadn't sounded like a croak, if her throat hadn't felt like a raw slab of meat, and if her legs hadn't seemed made of rubber.

Leaning closer to the bathroom mirror she decided that making herself look good would take more energy than she had at the moment. She'd stay in her room today, doing the latest regional reports from...where were they now? Albany? Hartford? No, it started with a *B*... Not Boston... She frowned and concentrated. "Baltimore!" she croaked. "I'm in Baltimore!"

She laughed even though part of her was wondering what she was laughing at. The other part didn't care, was just sort of floating. She hung onto the doorframe so she wouldn't float, too.

"You're getting delirious," she muttered in disapproval. "Stop it right now."

Her head was pounding, or was it her heart? No. She listened carefully. It was actually someone pounding on her hotel-room door.

Instead of leaving the support of the bathroom door-frame to look through the peephole, she yelled out, "Who is it?"

"It's me, Adam. I've got my regional report ready to give you."

"Just slide it under the door," she requested huskily.

"It's too thick to fit under the door," he replied. "Julia, are you all right? You sound strange."

"Uh, just a minute." She grabbed a robe from the closet across from the bathroom. Her fingers were trembling by the time she tied the robe's belt. Using every ounce of her willpower, she shakily undid the lock and opened the door a crack. She was balancing herself somewhat precariously with one hand on the wall and one hand on the doorknob.

"Are you all right?" Adam repeated.

"Fine. Just busy. Thanks for bringing me your report." She held out one hand for it and immediately began to sway. She closed her eyes as the walls began swirling.

"You're sick!" she heard Adam exclaim.

A second later she felt herself being swept off her feet and into his arms. Keeping her eyes closed, she let her hand rest against his shoulder. She didn't even care where he was taking her. She just didn't want to think anymore.

He set her down on something soft...the bed? She reached out an inquiring hand. Her fingers bumped into something solid and warm. His thigh? Was that the feel of denim under her fingers? It was certainly the feel of rock-hard muscle. She gave a half smile.

Before she could investigate further, Adam lifted her hand to his lips and kissed her trembling fingers. "Tell me where it hurts," he coaxed.

"All over."

He put his hand on her forehead. "You're burning up!" She turned away restlessly.

"We've got to call a doctor."

She didn't care anymore. She vaguely heard Adam talking to someone but couldn't muster the strength to concentrate on what he was saying. He sounded worried, though. He had a nice voice. Had she ever noticed that before? Nice voice and nice thighs. She was definitely delirious here. She hadn't said that out loud had she?

"What did I say?" she demanded querulously.

"Nothing." Adam hung up the phone. "A doctor will be here in fifteen minutes."

"Fine. You can leave now." One last rational segment of her mind knew she had to get rid of him before she blabbed something she shouldn't.

"Independent to the last, hmm?" he noted as he stroked her damp hair away from her forehead.

"I'm not in the mood for company."

"I'm not company."

She opened her eyes and had to blink several times before being able to focus on Adam's face. Nice eyes too, she noted hazily. Nice blue eyes. She remembered the first time she'd seen his eyes. They hadn't been filled with this warmth then, though. Was all that feeling for her? Maybe her vision was being affected by her fever. She closed her eyes again, too tired to figure it out, and too sick to argue with him about leaving.

She felt the mattress sway as he got up. So, he was taking her advice and going. Good. She heard a door close and panicked. She was alone now? That's what she wanted, right? She could cope, couldn't she?

Adam stood at the foot of the bed and stared in dismay as a single tear slid out from under Julia's closed eyelids and ran down her pale cheek.

"Hey, it'll be all right," he murmured reassuringly. He took the cold washcloth, which he'd gotten from the bathroom, and placed it on her forehead. "The doctor will be here soon and he'll give you something to make you feel better."

Julia made no reply. She wasn't even embarrassed at having been caught crying. She was feeling too ill to care.

When the doctor arrived a short time later he did a quick but thorough examination before proclaiming it to be a virus and prescribing antibiotics. "Is she allergic to anything?" the doctor asked Adam. "Penicillin?"

"I'm not sure," Adam said.

The doctor tried asking Julia about allergies, but she just looked at him blankly and mumbled something unintelligible before closing her eyes again.

"She's got a sister in Boston," Adam said. "I could call her and ask her about allergies."

"Do that. I'll write out both prescriptions on one form, but you'll only be able to fill one or the other. If you can't find out about allergies to penicillin, then have the second prescription filled. I've written it down here."

Scribbled was more like it, Adam thought as he looked down at the prescription note.

"Call me again tomorrow if that fever isn't down," the doctor said. "It's probably just a twenty-four-hour bug, virulent but not long lasting. Give her aspirin or an aspirin substitute every four hours in addition to the antibiotic."

"Thanks." Adam closed the door on the doctor and then tried to get his thoughts in order. It was no use asking Julia for her sister's name or phone number, he'd have to find it himself. He caught sight of her personal-agenda book sitting on the dresser by the TV. When he turned to the page listing numbers to use in an emergency, he found two listings. One was for a Mr. and Mrs. Brinkman in Phoenix, her mother and stepfather presumably. The second was for Patti Delaney in Boston. He turned to look at Julia. She appeared to be sleeping, so he went into the bathroom and used the phone in there so he wouldn't disturb her.

"Mrs. Delaney, this is Adam MacKenzie. I'm a friend of your sister, Julia."

"Has something happened to Julia?" he heard the young woman anxiously ask.

"She's got a bad case of the flu, but I've already had a doctor come look at her. He's prescribed some medication, but I don't know if Julia is allergic to penicillin. That's why I'm calling you."

"No, she's not allergic. Are you sure she's going to be okay?"

"I'll be staying with her to make sure she is okay," he stated firmly.

"Where are you calling from?"

"Baltimore." Adam gave Patti the name and phone number of the hotel.

"You're staying there with Julia?"

"While she's sick, yes."

"Have her call me as soon as she's feeling better."

"I'll do that."

Adam then called a bellboy and, for a sizable tip, had him take the prescription to a nearby pharmacy.

He had to wake Julia up to give her the medication.

She complained peevishly. "Go away." When he didn't, she turned onto her back and noticed the bottle he held in one hand. She gave him a suspicious look. "What's that?"

"Antibiotics. The doctor prescribed them for you."

"What doctor?"

"The doctor that was here half an hour ago looking at you. Don't you remember?"

She frowned. "I'm not sure."

"Don't worry about it now. Just take these two pills." He helped her sit up and held the glass of water to her lips. "Good girl. Now lie back and get some more sleep."

"You don't have to stay," she murmured.

"I know. Close your eyes and sleep."

Adam sank into one of the two chairs in the room and watched her. Her face was pale, but two bright spots of color stood out on her cheeks. She still wore the robe she'd had on when he'd first come to the door. Maybe he should have taken it off. Was she too hot in it?

His eyes strayed down her body. The nightgown she wore beneath the robe appeared to have more lace than material. Taking a deep breath, he decided he'd better leave well enough alone for the time being. At least the robe covered her. Tilting his head back, Adam stared at the ceiling and willed his hormones to settle down.

As if his conscience weren't giving him enough trouble as it was—lusting after a woman when she was incapacitated with the flu—he got a phone call a few minutes later from Julia's mother. He'd already moved the phone onto the other queen-size bed to get it as far away from Julia as possible. He grabbed it before the ringing could wake her.

"Hello?"

"I'd like to speak to Julia Trent please."

"I'm sorry, she's unavailable at the moment," he said in a quiet undertone. "Can I give her a message?"

"This is her mother. Are you Mr. MacKenzie?"

"Yes."

"My younger daughter called me and told me that Julia's sick."

"As I told Patti, it's just a bad case of the flu. I wouldn't have called at all, but I just wanted to make certain that Julia wasn't..."

"...allergic to penicillin. Yes, I know. Patti told me that. How long have you known Julia, Mr. MacKenzie?"

He settled back against the headboard. It looked as if this call might take awhile. "Please call me Adam. And I've known her for several weeks now."

"I hope you can understand a mother's concern at hearing about a phone call from a strange man telling us that my daughter is ill. I realize Julia is able to take care of herself under usual conditions, but I worry about her. It's only natural. You can understand that, can't you?"

"Certainly. But I can assure you that your daughter's in safe hands with me." Adam went on to talk with Julia's mother, allaying her fears, answering her questions without hesitation.

The sound of Adam's voice gradually sank into Julia's consciousness. She opened her eyes. "What did you say?" she asked groggily. Then she realized he wasn't talking to her; he was talking on the phone. "Who are you talking to?"

"Your mother," he answered.

"You're kidding, right?"

"Nope." He handed her the phone. "Say hi."

"Hello?"

"Julia, it's your mother, dear. I'm so sorry to hear you're sick. Promise me you'll take care of yourself and follow the doctor's instructions. That Adam of yours sounds like such a nice man. I'm so relieved there's someone looking out for you. You need someone like that in your life. But we'll talk about that later. For now, just rest. I'll call you again tomorrow."

"What was that all about?" she demanded as Adam took the phone from her and hung it up.

He shrugged. "I guess your mom was worried about you."

"How did she know I was sick?"

"Patti told her."

It was hard, but Julia was determined to follow this through. "And how did Patti know I was sick?"

"I had to call her and make sure you weren't allergic to penicillin."

"You called Patti?"

"That's right. I found her number in your personal-agenda book."

"What did she say?"

"That she hopes you're feeling better soon, and she wants you to call her. She sounded worried about you."

"And she promptly called my mom in Phoenix and told her I was sick in a hotel room somewhere with a strange man. Great."

"Your mom sounds like a nice lady."

"She worries too much."

"She said you'd say that," Adam noted.

"How long did you talk to her?"

"Long enough for us to get to know each other a little."

"Why?"

"Why what?"

"Why did you want to get to know my mom better? Trying to fill in the missing clues to my background?"

He shook his head at her. "You're getting delirious again."

"What do you mean *again*? What did I say?"

"Something about me having a nice voice and nice thighs, but other than that, nothing much. Are you blushing?"

"It's the fever," she muttered. "Look, you can go now. I appreciate your help, but I'll be okay."

Adam shook his head. "You're still running a fever, and you're still too weak to manage by yourself."

"Fine. Then maybe Maria can come help me."

"Maria flew back to Chicago earlier this morning."

"Oh. I forgot."

"Stop worrying and try and get some sleep."

"I've been doing nothing but sleep for the past three hours," she grumbled.

"You needed the rest. You're exhausted. You've been working too hard."

"No lectures, please."

"Okay, how about a Marx Brothers movie instead? There's one on TV this afternoon."

"Is it afternoon already?"

He nodded.

She looked horrified. "I have to get up. I can't stay in bed all day. I've got work to do. I'm supposed to get all those reports into the express mail so Helen will have them Monday morning.''

''I'll call her and tell her you're sick,'' Adam offered.

''No!''

''Then you call her.''

''No.''

''Are you always this stubborn when you're sick?''

''I'm feeling much better now.''

''Sure you are,'' he said disbelievingly.

She sat up, pushed the covers away and swung her feet down onto the floor.

''What do you think you're doing?'' he demanded.

''Getting up.''

''You do and you'll only fall down again.''

''I did not fall down.''

''Because I caught you in time.''

''You're exaggerating.'' She pushed up from the bed and stood up, giving him a triumphant look. ''There, see?''

She took two steps before she started swaying. For some reason her knees refused to hold her upright. It felt as if all her bones had turned to mush. It felt as if she were going to fall flat on her face.

Adam slid his arm around her waist and supported her. ''I see, all right, Wonder Woman. You're not ready to save the world just yet. Back to bed.''

She shook her head.

''I mean it, Julia. You're in no shape to be up yet.''

''I need to use the bathroom,'' she said with as much dignity as she could manage under the situation.

''Why didn't you just say so?'' He helped her the short distance to the bathroom. ''I'll wait for you outside.''

''Go turn on your Marx Brothers movie. I'll call you when I'm done.''

Aside from using the facilities, she also rinsed her mouth out with mouthwash and splashed cold water on her flushed face. She wanted to do something with her hair, which was up in a drunken topknot, but ran out of energy. Besides, the walls were doing their dancing routine again. She opened the door and Adam was there in a second. He took one look at her pale face, then picked her up and carried her back to bed.

She leaned on the pillow with a sigh of relief. It felt good to be horizontal again. She waited for Adam to make some sort of I-told-you-so comment, but he didn't say a word. He just kept right on watching the Marx Brothers movie. And so did she, until she drifted off to sleep once more.

The next time she woke, she was surprised to find that she felt hungry. She hadn't eaten much for dinner last night, just a light salad, and she hadn't had anything for breakfast.

"Lunch time," Adam announced as he wheeled in a room-service cart. "Chicken soup. Guaranteed to fix whatever ails you."

He helped her sit up and stuffed more pillows behind her. Then he sat down next to her with the bowl of soup in one hand and a spoon in the other. "Okay, open wide."

"Adam . . ."

"Good, good." He slipped a spoonful of soup inside her mouth.

She swallowed it and opened her mouth to speak. "I . . ."

He slipped in another spoonful of soup.

She swallowed that one, too, and spoke again. " . . . can do it . . ."

Another spoonful went in.

" . . . myself!"

"And deprive me of all this fun? No way. Okay, open wide; here comes the plane. . . ." He moved the spoon and made propeller-type noises as he aimed the soup toward her mouth.

"Let me guess. Is this the way you feed your nieces and nephews?"

He nodded and slid the spoon into her open mouth.

She grabbed his hand in hers before he could return the empty spoon for yet another helping. "I'm not a five-year-old," she said after swallowing the tasty soup.

He looked down at the creamy skin showing between the generous part of her robe. "I know," he said huskily.

"I can feed myself."

"We'll compromise. I'll hold the bowl. You can take charge of the spoon." He moved the bowl closer to make it easier for her and harder for himself. His arm was now so close to the curve of her breast that he could practically feel every breath she took. He sighed and tightened his grip on the bowl.

It was inevitable that sooner or later she'd lean forward for that last spoonful of soup. When she did, the motion caused her breast to brush against his arm. They both froze at the contact.

If Julia thought she'd felt warm before, it was nothing compared to what she felt now. She was burning up inside. It was a sudden fire, a sudden need.

Their eyes met, tangling as they wished their bodies could. The visual exchange reflected all the heat, all the desire, that the unexpectedly intimate contact had generated. Messages were passing between them at the speed of light, each one stronger and more erotic than the last—going straight from his heart to hers.

The spoon Julia had been holding fell back into the almost empty bowl. The clattering sound shattered the heavy silence and broke the spell binding them together.

Julia was the first to look away. "Uh, I guess I'm done with the soup," she awkwardly murmured.

Adam didn't say anything. He didn't trust his voice. He was done, too, almost done in by what had just transpired. After that he made a point of trying to keep his distance.

Julia tried pretending that nothing had happened. She also pretended to be asleep. She tried to direct her thoughts toward work, but it was no use. She could only focus on

Adam. He'd been with her all day and half the evening now. Normally she hated for anyone to see her when she was ill. She felt too much like a turtle without its shell—unable to protect herself, too vulnerable. And then there was the vanity factor—she looked like a washed-out ghost when she was sick.

But today she hadn't cared. Adam had made her feel comfortable...until his arm had brushed against her. Then he'd made her feel all achy and soft inside. It's the flu, she tried telling herself. Blame it all on the flu.

Her thoughts wandered. It felt kind of nice to be taken care of for a change, to be looked after. She wasn't used to it. She was much more accustomed to offering help than accepting it. Being on the receiving end was okay, she supposed, providing she didn't get too used to it.

She was drifting off, somewhere between sleep and a fever-induced stupor, when Adam abruptly declared, "I'm staying the night. You might as well get used to the idea."

Six

———

What, no argument?" Adam said.

"Would it do me any good?" Julia countered unsteadily.

"No."

"Then why should I waste my energy arguing?"

"Your fever must be going up again."

And it continued to go up as the night went on. Adam placed another call to the doctor, who told him that it was normal for a fever to go up at night and to keep Julia on the aspirin substitute. The fever should break by morning.

Julia slept through the worst of it. Adam had just managed to fall asleep himself when he was awakened by the sound of her mumbling. In a flash he jumped out of the other queen-size bed and came to her side.

"What's wrong?" he asked softly.

"Hot. I'm hot. Off." She tugged on the lapels of her robe.

"Take it easy. I'll take it off for you." It was a long and drawn-out process for Adam, who was having trouble getting the knot in the robe's sash undone. His hands were all thumbs as he eventually got that done and moved on to slip the robe from her shoulders. The lacy nightgown wanted to come with it.

He swallowed and tried again. This time he managed to get her arms out of the robe. Now all he had to do was tug the damn robe out from under her. It was a thin silky thing, thank God, which made it easier. But as he touched her, he realized that Julia's nightgown was damp with sweat. She was shivering.

"Damn it!" He knew what had to be done. She had to change into something dry. He looked around. A new nightgown. That's the first thing he should do. No, first he should cover her back up with the sheet. He did. But she just shoved it off again.

Realizing that he was fighting a losing battle on that front, he began looking for a replacement nightgown. Unfortunately the other three he found in the hotel-room drawer were even flimsier than the lacy one she had on. They might be cool, but they were just too damn sexy for his peace of mind. He had to put something more substantial on her, but something that wouldn't make her too warm.

A T-shirt would do the trick. Unfortunately he couldn't find one in either the closet or drawers. Wait, hadn't she bought one in St. Louis? After a little further searching he found the T-shirt, still in the bag. He held it up, silently praising its extra-large size. It would do fine.

Now the next problem was getting her out of what she had on. Normally he would have been more than pleased to have had this opportunity with Julia, but he knew she was defenseless, and he felt protective of her. He also wanted her, which made for a conflicting state of affairs.

He was a pro at problem-solving—so what was the most efficient, gentlemanly way of getting her out of that nightgown? He studied the garment as if it were an engineering puzzle. The nightgown appeared to unfasten with a series of bow ties down the front. Okay. He could handle that. He wanted to handle her....

"Bad choice of words, MacKenzie," he muttered.

Maybe he should ask for her help here.

"Julia, we've got to get you into a fresh nightgown, okay?"

"Hot," she muttered fretfully.

"I know you're hot." So am I, he thought to himself. "You'll be cooler in a minute. No, wait a second!" But he was too late, she'd already shoved the straps of her nightgown down off her shoulders. "Ah, hell." He pulled her into a sitting position and gently tugged the oversized T-shirt over her head. And not a moment too soon, because her lacy nightgown pooled at her waist. He guided her hands into the T-shirt's armholes. Unfortunately the nightgown needed to be loosened more before it could be lifted over her head. He tried to hurry as he reached under the cotton material of the T-shirt to undo the lacy bows of her nightgown. His hands brushed against her skin, and he felt as hot as she did.

She opened her eyes and looked at him. "Adam?"

"Yes?"

"What are you doing?"

"Putting a T-shirt on you."

For some reason she smiled. "Oh."

Swearing softly, he struggled with the last bow. When she lifted one hand, he thought she was either going to push him away or help him. But instead she pressed his head against her now bared breast. "I like that," she murmured unsteadily.

Sweat popped out on Adam's forehead. He liked it, too. He muttered her name like a man who'd reached the end of his rope.

She arched her back, thrusting more of her breast into the cupping palm of his hand. "Mmm."

Adam sternly told himself that she wasn't responsible for her actions. He reminded himself that she was in his care, that she was sick, for God's sake. Then he realized that his hand was cupping her, caressing her as if his fingers had a mind and a conscience of their own. Damn, she felt so good that he hated to stop. But stop he had to.

He pulled his hand away, tugged the nightgown out from under her hips, yanked it up over her head and pulled the T-shirt down, telling himself that he hadn't noticed the brief bikini underwear she was wearing. The entire episode had only taken a few minutes, but he felt as if he'd aged several years. Restraint might be good for the soul, but it sure wreaked havoc on the body.

While Adam stood next to the bed, his hands clenched, his entire body tense and aroused, Julia turned on her side, slipped her hand under her cheek like a little girl, and promptly fell asleep again.

Adam wasn't as lucky. He wasn't able to get back to sleep for some time after that, until just before sunrise. It was only a few hours after that that the sound of the phone ringing woke him. Forgetting where he was for a second, he grabbed the phone and mumbled hello.

"I'm sorry. I must have the wrong number. I'm trying to reach Julia Trent's room."

It was Helen calling. He recognized her voice. Damn. What should he do now? "Good morning, Helen. It's Adam. Julia's not feeling very well, so I came over this morning to check on her."

"Oh."

Adam thought Helen sounded surprised. She recovered quickly though. "I'm sorry to hear Julia's not well. I wanted to talk to her about Intercorp's New Orleans office. Your schedule has been changed and you'll all be going to New Orleans instead of Cleveland at the end of next week."

"I'll give her the message."

"You mean she's too ill to come to the phone? I hope this doesn't mean she's not going to be able to travel on Monday. I'll have to get a substitute if that's the case. Will she be well enough by Monday?"

"Your concern overwhelms me, Helen," he noted mockingly.

"I'm a bottom liner, Adam. And the bottom line is that if Julia is sick I've got to find a replacement and find one fast."

"Is that Helen?" a suddenly wide-awake Julia demanded. At Adam's nod, she said, "Give me the phone!"

Before doing so, he noted that Julia's fever appeared to have broken. Her eyes were clear this morning and her voice was less husky and more lucid than it had been last night. When he held out the receiver she practically grabbed it from his hand.

"Helen, it's Julia."

"You don't sound very good. What is it, a cold?"

"No, just a touch of the flu. I'll be fine."

"Are you sure? You're traveling to Pittsburgh tomorrow afternoon, and then you've got two intensive days of seminars there."

"I'm sure. My voice just sounds a little raspy, but the antibiotics are working."

"It was nice of Adam to stop by this morning and check in on you. It's a little early for a visit, isn't it?" Helen noted casually.

"Not really. You know us, Helen," she joked weakly. "Always working, even early on Sunday morning."

"How could you be working? Adam told me you were too ill to come to the phone."

"He exaggerates. Really, I'm fine."

"Well, I must admit that I'm relieved to hear that you'll be able to give your seminars. I'm counting on you, Julia."

"I know you are."

"Good. Did you get a chance to send out the Baltimore report yesterday?"

Guilt hit her. "No, I'm sorry I didn't get that out. I'll get it out first thing in the morning."

"That means I'll get it Tuesday instead of Monday."

"I know. I'm sorry."

Helen sighed. "I'll have to work around it. Call me when you get to Pittsburgh."

Julia hung up the phone feeling as if she'd really let Helen down. It was only then that she realized she was wearing some sort of T-shirt instead of her nightgown. She frowned. She didn't remember changing clothes.

Adam saw that frown and braced himself for the fireworks that were bound to follow.

"What happened last night?" she asked with calm caution.

"Nothing."

"I was not wearing this T-shirt when I went to sleep last night."

"Not the first time you went to sleep, no."

"Then how did I come to be wearing it this morning?"

He grinned. "Now *there's* a story."

"I don't want to hear a story, I want to hear the truth and quickly."

"You don't remember last night?"

The memory of some very heated dreams crossed her mind. They *had* been dreams, hadn't they? "You spent the night?"

Adam nodded. "You woke up in the middle of the night. Your fever had gotten higher."

"And?"

"And you decided you didn't want to wear your robe any longer. Or your nightgown either for that matter. You took them off, and I helped."

Don't blush, she told herself, but it was no use. She could feel the heat stealing into her face, staining her cheeks.

"How *exactly* did you help?" she demanded. To herself she added, What did you see? What did you touch? What did you do? What did I do? Had her dreams been real? The questions blazed through her head.

"Relax." He brushed his hand down her flushed cheek.

"I will once you've answered my question."

"I exchanged your nightgown for the T-shirt," he said matter-of-factly. "You were properly covered at all times," he added.

"How did you manage that?"

"It wasn't easy, but I managed. I'm nothing if not creative."

"That's what I'm afraid of," she muttered.

"What did you say?"

"Nothing. I think I'll go take a shower now."

"Whoa. You're not fully recovered yet. I wouldn't go jumping out of bed if I were you."

"You're not me."

"What's the hurry?"

"I've got things to do."

"The first of which is to rest and recover your strength."

"I've already done that. I've got to get those reports out to Helen. I let her down by not getting them out to her on time."

"You were sick."

She shook her head. "That's no excuse."

"Julia, everyone gets sick at one time or another. It happens."

"Not to me, it doesn't."

"Why should it happen to the rest of us and not to you?"

"Because I'm supposed to be..." She broke off, unable to find the words to continue.

"You're supposed to be what?" he questioned. "Stronger? Better? Tougher?"

"You don't understand. Helen was depending on me. She needed me to be on time."

"And what about your needs? Is your need to please Helen so great that you're willing to forgo all your other needs?"

"A lot is riding on how well I do on this project. This is my chance to prove myself, and I can't afford to make any mistakes." She paused, wondering why she was trying to justify herself to him. "Would you please hand me my robe. I'd like to get up and take a shower."

He handed her the robe without mentioning the fact that he'd seen her wearing less.

"I'm much better now," she assured him. "I appreciate your calling a doctor, but as you can see, I'm fine. You can go back to your own room and do whatever it is you normally do on your Sunday off." Julia gritted her teeth and vowed not to let her shakiness show. She did feel better. She was just a little weak—an aftereffect from the fever. Her legs would soon regain their normal strength; she wouldn't give them a choice. She made it to the bathroom entirely under her own steam, an accomplishment she was inordinately proud of. "I'll see you tomorrow, Adam."

"Okay." He knew when he'd been dismissed, he noted ruefully as she closed the bathroom door in his face. That didn't mean he had to obey. She'd told him to do what he'd normally do on his Sunday off. So he picked up the newspaper that the hotel had left outside in the hallway and he began reading the funny papers. He wasn't about to leave, wondering if she'd slipped in the shower. Besides he wasn't done talking to her yet.

Julia stepped out of the shower feeling much more like her old self. She was determined to ignore the lingering signs of weakness. Instead she found herself wondering how Adam had managed to keep her covered while switching her nightgown for a T-shirt. She tugged the lapels of the hotel's toweling robe closer together. While brushing her teeth, another thought hit her. Had she said anything last night, anything that might have been less than . . . prudent? Fevers affected her that way. Her defenses tumbled, and she babbled.

No, if she'd said anything, Adam would have taken great delight in reminding her of it first thing this morning. Instead he'd gone out of his way to reassure her and make her feel comfortable. Not exactly the actions of a man with just lust on his mind.

In fact, he'd been extremely caring, not just physically but emotionally as well. She left the bathroom, absently rubbing her damp hair with a towel, only to halt in her tracks when she saw Adam sprawled across the spare bed, reading the Sunday comics.

"You're still here."

He nodded. "That's right."

"Why?"

He took her by the arm and led her over to a chair near the window. "Anyone ever told you you've got a very suspicious nature? No? Then let me be the first."

She wished he had been the first—the first man to pursue her, the first to make love to her. Maybe then it wouldn't have mattered that she cared too much, if she'd cared for the right man. She sighed. It was too complicated to work out this early in the morning.

"Here, I got breakfast for you. Poached eggs and toast." He held out the chair for her. "Sit."

She sat, grudgingly. "You enjoy ordering people around, don't you?"

He nodded and sat across from her. "Want to hear what else I enjoy?" he leaned forward to ask huskily.

She found herself nodding before she had time to stop herself.

He moved closer yet, until his lips were only a few inches away. His blue eyes were dark with desire as he murmured, "Scrambled eggs."

"Wha...at?"

Her flustered response brought a smile to his lips. "I enjoy scrambled eggs. But only after I've had my morning kiss."

It was the only warning she received, the only warning she needed. She had time to move away. She didn't. She thought she probably should, but while she was deliberating, he kissed her. And then logic went out the nearby window.

He hadn't shaved, and the shadowy stubble rasped against her skin as he nibbled on her lips. The friction was primitively sensual. She felt his hands caressing her face, his thumbs tenderly stroking the corners of her mouth. His touch reflected the combination of gentleness and strength already present in the kiss. He was coaxing her to respond, convincing her of the rightness of it all.

Her lips parted, and she returned the kiss. The table still separated them, and it soon became a nuisance. Adam dealt with it by getting up and moving around it, all without removing his lips from hers. Putting his hands on Julia's shoulders, he pulled her up from the chair and into his arms.

The embrace was now much more satisfying for both of them. It was also more provocative. They were pressed together from shoulder to thigh. There was magic in the way he held her, passion in the way his hands caressed her. He soon grew impatient with the thick terry-cloth robe that prevented him from touching the smooth silkiness of her skin.

Julia, too, grew impatient. She wanted him to touch her; she needed to touch him. Her fingers restlessly ran over his shoulders. When he bent his head to kiss his way from her temple down around to the nape of her neck, she slid her fingers through his dark hair. She was surprised by its texture, so soft compared to the seductive roughness of his beard.

He rewarded her explorations by turning his head and nuzzling the juncture between her throat and her shoulder, tantalizing her with his tongue. The creamy slopes of her breasts weren't far away now. He slid his hands over her, and Julia shivered with pleasure.

He turned with her in his arms. Before she knew what had happened she was lying on the bed with him. It had happened so quickly she didn't have time to protest. Her hazy thoughts were further clouded by pleasure as Adam loosened the lapel on her robe. Then he was touching her as she'd longed for him to touch her. It was as if he'd touched her this way before.

She suddenly went very still. With a flash of insight, she realized that he *had* touched her this way before—and she'd loved it then just as she loved it now. Those hadn't been dreams last night! That realization gave her the strength to pull away from him.

"No!" She turned her head to one side, away from his tempting lips. "We have to stop."

"Stop?" He nibbled his way across her throat. "Why?"

"Because that was no dream last night. You've done this before," she accused him.

He looked at her in confusion. "Done what?"

Made my blood pound, made my heart stop, she thought. Aloud she said, "You know what."

"You mean this?" He ran his index finger from her collarbone down the valley between her breasts.

"That's exactly what I mean." She broke free and sat up, clutching the lapels of her robe. "You took advantage of me."

"When?"

"Last night."

He propped himself up on one elbow and shook his head. "I already told you about last night."

She got off the bed. Her legs were a bit shaky, but they held her up. She silently cursed her own weakness, not so much her physical weakness as her emotional one. This wasn't supposed to be happening again. She shouldn't have let Adam kiss her, let alone embrace her. She knew better

SILHOUETTE®

 **PRESENTS** 🖤

A Real Sweetheart of a Deal!

6 FREE GIFTS

PEEL BACK THIS CARD AND SEE WHAT YOU CAN GET! THEN...

Complete the Hand Inside ➤

It's easy! To play your cards right, just match this card with the cards inside.

Turn over for more details...

Incredible, isn't it? Deal yourself in right now and get 6 fabulous gifts ABSOLUTELY FREE.

1. 4 BRAND NEW SILHOUETTE DESIRE® NOVELS—FREE!

Sit back and enjoy the excitement, romance and thrills of four fantastic novels. You'll receive them as part of this winning streak!

2. A LOVELY BRACELET WATCH—FREE!

You'll love your elegant bracelet watch—this classic LCD quartz watch is a perfect expression of your style and good taste—and it's yours free as an added thanks for giving our Reader Service a try!

3. AN EXCITING MYSTERY BONUS—FREE!

And still your luck holds! You'll also receive a special mystery bonus. You'll be thrilled with this surprise gift. It will be the source of many compliments as well as a useful and attractive addition to your home.

PLUS

THERE'S MORE. THE DECK IS STACKED IN YOUR FAVOR. HERE ARE THREE MORE WINNING POINTS. YOU'LL ALSO RECEIVE:

4. FREE HOME DELIVERY

Imagine how you'll enjoy having the chance to preview the romantic adventures of our Silhouette heroines in the convenience of your own home! Here's how it works. Every month we'll deliver 6 new Silhouette Desire® novels right to your door. There's no obligation to buy, and if you decide to keep them, they'll be yours for only $2.24* each—that's a savings of 26¢ per book! And there's no charge for postage and handling—there are no hidden extras!

5. A MONTHLY NEWSLETTER—FREE!

It's our special "Silhouette" Newsletter—our members' privileged look at upcoming books and profiles of our most popular authors.

6. MORE GIFTS FROM TIME TO TIME—FREE!

It's easy to see why you have the winning hand. In addition to all the other special deals available only to our home subscribers, when you join the Silhouette Reader Service, you can look forward to additional free gifts throughout the year.

SO DEAL YOURSELF IN—YOU CAN'T HELP BUT WIN!

*In the future, prices and terms may change, but you always have the opportunity to cancel your subscription. Sales taxes applicable in N.Y. and Iowa.

You'll Fall In Love With This Sweetheart Deal From Silhouette!

SILHOUETTE READER SERVICE™
FREE OFFER CARD

4 FREE BOOKS • FREE BRACELET WATCH • FREE MYSTERY BONUS • FREE HOME DELIVERY • INSIDER'S NEWSLETTER • MORE SURPRISE GIFTS

YES! Deal me in. Please send me four free Silhouette Desire novels, the bracelet watch and my free mystery bonus as explained on the opposite page. If I'm not fully satisfied I can cancel at any time, but if I choose to continue in the Reader Service I'll pay the low members-only price each month.

225 CIS JAY2
(U-S-D-09/89)

First Name   Last Name

PLEASE PRINT

Address   Apt.

City   State   Zip Code

Offer limited to one per household and not valid to current Silhouette Desire subscribers. All orders subject to approval.

SILHOUETTE NO RISK GUARANTEE

- There is no obligation to buy—the free books and gifts remain yours to keep.
- You'll receive books before they're available in stores.
- You may end your subscription at any time—by sending us a note or a shipping statement marked "cancel" or by returning any unopened shipment to us by parcel post at our expense.

PRINTED IN U.S.A.

Remember! To win this hand, all you have to do is place your sticker inside and DETACH AND MAIL THE CARD BE-LOW. You'll get four free books, a free bracelet watch and a mystery bonus.

BUT DON'T DELAY!
MAIL US YOUR LUCKY CARD TODAY!

If card is missing write to:
Silhouette Reader Service, 901 Fuhrmann Blvd., P.O. Box 1867, Buffalo, N.Y. 14269-1867

than to allow these kinds of feelings to grow. Yet here she was, still trembling from the pleasure of his caresses.

"I want you to leave," she said.

"No way." Now he sat up, too. "You're not getting off that easily. We have to talk about this."

"There's nothing to talk about."

"Don't give me that. Last night you may not have been responsible for your actions, but you can't use that excuse this morning. You were an equal participant in what just happened."

"What exactly *did* happen last night?"

"Let's just say that you let me know you enjoyed my touch."

"I was delirious," she said defensively.

"Which is why I didn't take you up on the invitation. But this morning you're as clearheaded as I am, probably more so, since I didn't sleep most of the night."

"I'm sorry if taking care of me was difficult for you," she said stiffly.

"I'll tell you what was difficult—not making love to you. Don't pretend that you don't feel the same way."

"I don't deny that there's a certain...sexual attraction at work here."

"What's between us is more than just sex. Not that just sex is bad," he added with a rakish grin, "but this is better, stronger. The question is, what are we going to do about it?"

"Nothing. I already told you that I don't mix business and pleasure."

"I know what you told me. Why don't you tell me the *real* reason. I know you're not as cool as you pretend to be. Why do you think you have to pretend with me?"

"Who says I'm pretending?"

"Come on. The way you kissed me, the way you came alive in my arms—that's the truth. Why are you afraid of it?"

"Because you're better at this than I am."

"Oh, I wouldn't say that," he drawled. "You're pretty fantastic."

"I'm referring to playing mind games, knowing what buttons to push, how to get the reaction you want."

"If I were able to get the reaction I want we'd both be on that bed right now, finishing what we started a few minutes ago."

"It's because I haven't given in that I've become a challenge to you, a problem for you to solve."

"Why are you so convinced I'm playing games with you?" he demanded impatiently. "Is it easier for you to think that than to face the fact that I could want more, feel more for you? Why are you so afraid of a little honest-to-God emotion? Why do you keep everyone at arm's length? Why do you act as if you don't care?"

"Because I care too much! There! Are you satisfied? Are you happy now? You've got your answer. The truth is that I can't afford to care."

"Why not? What's going to happen if you care too much?"

"What's happened before. I give everything, and then I get dumped. I learn by my mistakes."

"Let me get this straight. You don't want to get involved with me because you think I'm going to dump you?"

She shook her head. "It's not about you; it's about me. I can't take things lightly. It's all or nothing with me. You say that I only pretend to be cool. That's right, I do. I have to. And I can't afford to have you tugging at emotions that are better left alone. Sure there's an attraction between us, and you're curious about what it could be like. But once that curiosity was satisfied, you'd move on, and I'd be a wreck."

"Why should I move on?"

"Because you're the type of man who likes setting goals for himself. And once you've reached that goal, you set another. That's all I am to you, just another goal."

"So you're saying that I enjoy the thrill of the hunt more than I do the fox, is that it?"

"I suppose that's one way of putting it, yes."

"Bull!"

"I beg your pardon."

"And so you should. Credit me with some common sense. The hunt might have some things going for it, but they're paltry in comparison to having the warm and cuddly fox in your arms. Trust me." He paused a moment. "And I guess that's what it all boils down to in the end—a matter of trust. The best way to prove that I'm not playing games with you is to just stick around and not move on. Maybe then you'll see that it's okay to care, that I'm not going to abuse your trust in me."

"Maybe it's myself I don't trust more than you," she admitted unsteadily. "When I care, I care too much, *way* too much. I become someone I don't like very much, someone who puts up with more than I should, who does everything for someone else. I go overboard. Nothing is too much trouble. I keep trying harder and harder to please. And all I end up doing is alienating those I care about."

Adam had a hard time reconciling the woman he knew with the woman she was talking about. "Maybe you've just been caring for the wrong type."

"That's true, too."

"Aside from the fact that we're temporarily working together, what makes me the wrong type?"

Julia had to stop and think about that one for a minute. Nothing else came to mind. Adam wasn't anything like the brooding type she'd fallen for in the past, the type that needed lots of patience and understanding. He didn't really have any serious character defects that needed fixing. He might be unpredictable, but he wasn't unreliable or unstable. He went his own way, had his own way of looking at things, but he had no problems with self-identity. He knew who he was, knew what he wanted, and he went after it. She could attest to that.

So what *did* make him wrong for her? Maybe it was more that she felt *she* was wrong for *him*. She was the one with the problem, not him. Which left her where? Afraid to go forward and afraid to go back? Afraid of his motives? Afraid to really believe that he did care for her? Afraid to trust her judgment when it had failed her in the past? Afraid of caring too much and getting hurt again? Or all of the above?

"I don't know," she murmured.

"Well, I do. I've given this plenty of thought, you know," Adam said. "I wasn't expecting to feel this way about you, and I'll admit it confused me, too. I couldn't figure out what it was that kept drawing me to you. You're everything I'm not—quiet, cautious, ambitious. But somehow our differences seem to mesh, making me feel complete. I look at you and feel good inside. I also look at you and want you—want to take you to bed, want to hug you, want to protect you, want to laugh with you, want to be quiet with you. I'm not saying it isn't scary; I'm saying that it's special and worth taking risks for. If you really don't agree, if you don't feel that way too, then tell me. I may have a hard time believing you," he admitted truthfully, "but I'll listen."

She'd never had a man say these things to her, communicate with her so openly. She couldn't do less in return. Subterfuge and excuses had no place here. It was hard—very hard—because it was easier hiding behind glib words than baring her true feelings. But she was tired of the game playing.

So even though her fingers were trembling and her tongue felt glued to the roof of her mouth, she told him the truth. "I ..." She cleared her throat and started again. "I feel the same way." Once she'd started, the words came a little easier. "I think about you when I should be thinking about work, and when you kiss me, I can't think at all."

"Great."

She held up a cautioning hand. "I'm just not as sure about things as you are. As you said, I'm cautious. I know my weaknesses and I've learned to work around them. I can't honestly give you any promises. I don't *want* to feel this way. And it doesn't change the fact that we are still working together."

"And you don't mix business with pleasure."

"That's right."

"An obstacle but not an insurmountable problem. We're already more than halfway through this project. In a little less than three weeks we no longer will be working together. And I'll give you fair notice now—I'm not giving up."

Julia's family didn't give up, either—give up trying to find out about Adam. Patti called her the very next evening in Pittsburgh.

"How did you know where I was?" Julia asked, surprised to hear from her.

"Mom told me. Now I want you to tell me about this guy of yours."

"What guy of mine?"

"Adam Mac-something-or-other."

"Adam MacKenzie is a fellow seminar instructor."

"Mom says he was in your room when she called. She said it sounded as if he'd fallen for you. She said . . ."

Julia already knew how close her mom, *their* mom was to Patti and vice versa. She already knew that they talked to each other all the time, that they both agreed she was a hopeless cause. She didn't need her nose rubbed in it this way. "Is that why you called me, to tell me everything Mom said?"

"Of course not. I told you why I called. To find out all about this mystery man of yours. And to see how you were feeling, of course."

"Of course," Julia said dryly.

"Hey, I was worried about you, you know. Mom was too."

"I know Mom was worried, that's why I told her my itinerary for the next few days. She insisted."

"And when Mom insists, there's no fighting her."

"No, there isn't. You must have gotten that characteristic from her," Julia noted.

"I was just going to say the same about you," Patti retorted. "So tell me about Adam."

"I already told you . . ."

"Tell me why he was in your room."

"He was being a Good Samaritan and checking up on me."

"Good Samaritan, my foot. What's he look like?"

Julia was tempted to say that he was seventy and bald. She recognized Patti's tone of voice. She'd heard it before. It was her "matchmaking voice." "Adam's got brown hair and blue eyes."

"So he's good-looking? Unmarried? How old?"

"Yes. Yes. Mid-thirties."

"Why didn't you mention him when we had dinner here in Boston? Or better yet, why didn't you bring him along? I would've loved to have met him."

"We don't have that kind of relationship." At least not yet, Julia added to herself.

"Well, I suppose it's not a good idea to intimidate him by having him meet your family too soon. We wouldn't want to scare him off."

"He's not the type to scare easily."

"Mom said he sounded pretty responsible, not like some of the other guys you've known in the past."

"You make it sound like I've gone through a legion of men," Julia protested. "There have only been a few."

"But they've all been losers."

"Which is why I'm now concentrating on my career and learning to be responsible for my own happiness instead of searching for it in some man," she said tartly.

"You sound angry. I just want you to be happy, Julia."

"Then you'll have to let me find my own way. That goes for Mom, too."

After she'd hung up, she felt guilty for snapping at Patti. But Patti's views on her love life had hit a sore spot with her. Things had always come easily to Patti. Love had always come easily for her. She was good at making people happy. She was good at telling others how to live their lives.

Julia sighed. Just when she was starting to consider the possibility of pursuing this attraction between herself and Adam, Patti had to come along and dig up all her doubts again. Why couldn't she be more like her sister? Light-hearted, not too serious, not too intense.

Sometimes she wondered what Adam saw in her. But then he'd look at her in that special way of his and make her feel like the only woman in the world. He'd touch her hand and make her come alive. He'd smile at her and make her want to kiss him.

Where before she'd noted the passing of her days by what happened at work, now she marked the passage of time by her interaction with Adam. Where once she'd connected cities to the success of her seminars there, now she thought of them in connection to what had happened with Adam.

In Cincinnati they'd stayed at a suite hotel, where, in addition to the standard bedrooms and bathrooms, all the accommodations had private kitchens and sitting rooms with TV's and VCR's. Adam rented a tape of *Casablanca*, remembering from that first creativity seminar that it was her favorite. They'd shared a bowl of popcorn he'd made in the kitchen. He'd even handed her a Kleenex when she'd cried at the end of the movie. Ever since then he'd whisper to her, "At least we had Cincinnati" in a passable Bogey impersonation.

In New Orleans they'd talked of going to visit one of the plantation houses nearby, but Julia had had to cancel when Helen had requested that she take on an extra seminar. Still, they did manage to sneak in a ten-minute carriage ride through the French Quarter.

In Denver he'd slid two magazine articles under her door. One listed the ten best places to get a hot-fudge sundae in the United States; the other explored the relationship between chocolate and sexual gratification. He'd even made notes in the margin! Julia didn't know whether to laugh or run in the opposite direction. Just so long as she didn't run straight into his arms. Not yet. It was too soon.

Adam returned to Chicago only one weekend. Julia didn't return at all. She'd meant to, but something had always come up, one crisis or another.

So when she finally did arrive at Chicago's O'Hare airport it was only because the Intercorp project had finally been completed. It was early August now, and it was just as hot as it had been when she'd left in mid-June. The group's return was marked with congratulations from Helen and promises of a farewell party for Adam. His time with Dynamics was coming to an end.

Later that evening, as Julia walked into her apartment, she realized that her running days were just about over. There was no place to hide in the apartment, no place to get away from her own thoughts. On the road there had always been the distraction of the project and the heavy workload involved. There had been Maria, Larry and Karl to talk to. And Adam. Always Adam.

But here it was quiet. There weren't any distractions. There wasn't much furniture, either, she noted. She'd been meaning to do something about that, but there hadn't ever been enough time, and besides she didn't spend much time at the apartment. But it was something of a shock to realize she'd had the place for almost two years now and still hadn't bought a couch or a dining-room table and chairs. Had

Adam been right? Had she become so wrapped up with work, so obsessed with it that it prevented her from having to think, to deal, to cope with anything else?

But her job gave her a strong sense of identity, and that was something she'd desperately needed. Julia Trent, seminar instructor, didn't have personal problems. She was too busy coping with more important issues—the kind of issues that made her feel important, made her feel as if she was accomplishing something. She liked those feelings. It was better than feeling helpless, the way she had as a kid. No matter how she'd tried she hadn't been able to make her mother feel better after her father had taken off and deserted them.

She frowned. She didn't like to dwell on the past, although she seemed to be doing so more and more lately, which wasn't necessarily a good sign. She needed something else to think about. Removing a stack of project notes from her briefcase, she set to work. She didn't accomplish as much as she'd hoped to because thoughts of Adam kept getting in the way. What was he doing tonight? Would he call her?

At that very moment the phone rang.

"Whatcha doin'?"

Julia recognized Adam's voice right away, but to tease him she said, "Who is this?"

He sighed dramatically. "How quickly they forget."

"Wait a minute. It's coming back to me now. Aren't you the man who wears neon gym shoes and hula-dancer ties?"

"Yes, but never at the same time. At least, not so far. But now that you mention it, maybe I should wear them both for my last day at Dynamics tomorrow. What do you think?"

"I think you'd do well to wear slacks and a shirt in addition to just those gym shoes and tie."

"Party pooper."

"Sticks and stones may break my bones, but words will never hurt me," she recited in a singsong voice.

"I don't want to break your bones; I want to jump them."

"That's one of the things I admire most about you, Adam. Your subtlety."

"That and my nice thighs, right?"

She groaned. "You're never going to let me forget that, are you?"

"No. And I'm not going to let you forget me, either, Julia. Sleep tight and dream of me."

And so she did, but those dreams made her late to work the next morning, and she remained behind schedule for the rest of the day. She'd just cleared enough of a path through the paperwork piled on her desk to actually see the wooden surface beneath all the papers when Maria came to tell her that the party in honor of Adam's last day had started.

"I'll be right there," Julia promised.

"I'll wait for you. I know how you get when you're wrapped up with work. You lose all track of time."

"I seem to recall you once accusing me of being punctual to a fault. How can I be punctual if I lose all track of time?" The beeper from Julia's watch answered her own question for her. She smiled sheepishly. "Okay, so now you know my secret."

"I'm glad to see that you included this party in your schedule. You and Adam are obviously getting along better now."

"We get along fine."

"I noticed."

"What did you notice?" Julia countered quickly.

"No need to panic."

"I never panic. Don't you know that?"

"I've heard rumors to that effect, yes, but I've never believed them myself," Maria said.

"Gee, thanks," Julia retorted.

"Only idiots never panic, and I know you're no idiot."

"Isn't that something Adam said in one of his seminars?"

Maria nodded. "You know, I'm going to miss having him around."

"So am I," Julia admitted softly.

Seven

This is supposed to be a party," Adam whispered in Julia's ear. "Cheer up."

"I am cheered up. Can't you tell?"

He gently tipped up her chin and studied her lips. "Yes, there it is, that discreet smile, the one that says you're having a great time. I see it now, just there at the corner of your mouth." He shook his head in wry disbelief. "Don't know how I could have missed it before. I've been staring at your mouth for at least the past ten minutes now, remembering the feel of your lips beneath mine, the touch of your tongue...."

"You two seem deep in conversation. What are you talking about?" Helen asked.

Julia stiffened and hurriedly stepped back from Adam. She felt guilty without quite knowing why.

"We were just discussing our various techniques," Adam replied. "Our strong points. Things we do well and want to do even better."

Julia didn't say a word. She was concentrating all her efforts on trying not to blush. She felt like a silly schoolgirl. It wasn't a feeling she was accustomed to, nor one she welcomed.

"Well, Adam, it's back to the schoolroom for you. You must be eager to return to those lovely young coeds," Helen said.

"I've got a few weeks before I have to face that yet," he replied.

"Are you taking some vacation time?" Helen asked. "Going somewhere to recover from the frantic pace of this Intercorp assignment?"

"No, I plan on staying right here in Chicago for a change and enjoying some of the local beauty." He looked directly at Julia as he spoke.

The interplay was duly noted by Helen. "You two seem to be getting along much better than when you first left," she commented.

"You could say that," Adam agreed.

"So what's your secret?" Helen asked.

"Secret?" Julia almost choked on the fruit punch she was sipping. "What secret?"

"To getting along."

Realizing it was about time she take the conversation in hand, Julia reminded Helen, "Adam and I reached an understanding before we left Chicago."

"That's right," Adam agreed. "A little give, a little take, and we still have an understanding."

"The art of negotiating, hmm? Sounds good. Julia—" Helen took her by the arm "—I need to talk to you about those last reports you filed from San Francisco."

Julia spent the rest of the party talking business with Helen. It wasn't until Helen was called away on a phone call that Julia got to speak to Adam again.

"Are you enjoying the party?" she asked him.

"I'm enjoying it more now that you're back by my side."

"What?" she teased him. "You mean you missed me in between that belly-dancing routine and the gorilla with the singing telegram?"

"Let me guess, those were Karl's ideas, right?"

"What's wrong? Not quite your cup of tea?" Julia inquired.

"Depends who's doing the belly dancing. Now if it were you, I'd definitely be interested. But as it was, I was merely an impartial bystander. I did appreciate the gift, though."

"I'm glad. It wasn't easy coming up with something suitable. I mean, what can you give a creative problem-solver? Then we hit it. A better mousetrap."

"Complete with mechanical mice." He smiled. "Nice touch."

To Julia, his touch was more than nice as he ran his fingers across the back of her hand. It was the lightest of caresses, and she felt as if she were walking on air. It wasn't wise; it wasn't safe, but there didn't seem to be anything she could do about it. Except to try to keep her feet at least semiclose to the ground and to take things slowly.

But that was difficult to do when he was tugging her down the hallway toward an empty conference room. Once inside he said, "Do you know what time it is?"

She looked at her watch. "A little after five."

"That's right. And do you know what that means?"

"That I've still got an hour's worth of work to do in my office."

He shook his head. "It means that we're no longer working for the same company." He moved until she was backed up against the conference table. "There's no longer any threat of mixing business with pleasure." Leaning forward he put his hands on the table behind her, effectively pinning her in a seductive triangle formed by his arms. "Your time's just run out, and I can't wait a second longer to do this...."

He kissed her. It wasn't sweet and it wasn't short—it was hard and hungry. So was he. She could feel the need in him, not only in the taut arousal of his body, but in the aching intensity of his kiss. He wanted her, and he was making no effort to disguise that desire from her.

She wanted him, too. Her lips parted; her tongue dueled with his. The exchange was slick and sultry. Julia was swept away by the building excitement.

In a minute, she thought to herself. I'll stop this in a minute. But sweet heaven it felt so good. Her murmur of pleasure was swallowed by the kiss. The things he was doing to her with his tongue made her knees weak. This magic was too irresistible to fight. It was meant to be enjoyed.

Then Julia heard something. Startled, she opened her eyes and looked over Adam's shoulder in time to see Helen's disapproving expression as she stood in the hallway. A moment later, Helen had closed the door, once again leaving them alone.

"What's wrong?" Adam asked as Julia abruptly pulled away from him.

"I can't believe this!" she practically wailed. "I should know better! A conference room is no place to be fooling around."

"A bedroom would be better," he agreed.

"Helen saw us."

"So?"

"So. So?" Julia stuttered, something she never did. "So she saw us, Adam. She saw us kissing."

"So?" he repeated.

"So, she's my boss. What's she going to think?"

"That you've got good taste in men," he suggested.

"That I make a practice of fooling around in conference rooms."

"Come on, Julia. Don't you think you're overreacting just a bit here? From what I understand, Helen has known you for several years. She must know you're not the kind of

woman who usually fools around in conference rooms—or
any other place for that matter. Usually you're dependable,
responsible, reliable and all that other good stuff."

"I'd just have preferred that she not see us. It makes me
feel, I don't know, guilty somehow. Like I'm doing something I shouldn't. Which is true. I *was* doing something I
shouldn't. My behavior while in the office, or the conference room, or any other room at work, should be professional."

"It sounds like you've lifted that from an employee
manual or something."

"Actually it's a line from a management seminar I do on
professional etiquette," she admitted.

"I thought so. You know, life doesn't always turn out the
way we expect it to. It doesn't always fit into the various
situations we talk about in seminars. Sometimes it takes a
wild and crazy turn."

"Tell me about it," she said morosely.

Adam sighed. "Well, there's no doubt in my mind, Helen has definitely ruined the mood here. What do you say we
go to my place?"

"I wasn't kidding when I said I had a lot of work to finish before I can leave. And besides, I'm not ready to rush
into anything." She gave him an exasperated look. "We
haven't even had a date yet."

"Date? You want to date? Fine. I can do that. How about
tomorrow night, Friday night? I'll pick you up at six. I already have your address and phone number. If you're going
to be late, call me. I wrote my number in your personal-
agenda book."

"Sure of yourself, aren't you?" she retorted.

"One of us has to be."

Throughout the next day, Julia waited for Helen to make
some comment about what she'd seen. Finally, a little after
four, Helen called Julia into her office.

"I just wanted to tell you that I appreciate the great job you did on the Intercorp project," Helen said. "Would you still be interested in a position as project leader?"

"Yes, of course."

"I thought I'd ask, after what I saw yesterday."

"I can explain," Julia said, even though she wasn't sure exactly *how* she'd explain it.

Luckily Helen let her off the hook. "There's no need. I assume you were caught up in the party spirit and that it was a momentary lapse. These things happen. I know you're dedicated to your career and won't let anything distract you from your goals. Your goals haven't changed, have they?"

"No."

"Good. I'm glad to hear that. Well, I'm running late. We'll talk more next week. You'll have the follow-up report on Intercorp done by Monday, right?"

"Monday?" Julia repeated, thinking of the pile of work yet to be done on that report.

"Is there a problem with that?" Helen demanded.

"No, no problem. It will be done by Monday."

"Good. Have a nice weekend."

"Thanks." Julia didn't know about *nice*, but it would certainly be a *busy* weekend. "You, too."

Not for the first time Julia was glad that her apartment was located only twenty minutes away from the office. If Adam was picking her up at six she didn't have much time to get ready. The phone was ringing when she opened her door. She grabbed it in a hurry.

"You sound out of breath. Did you just get in?" Adam asked her.

"Yes."

"I wanted to remind you to wear something casual. Jeans if you have them and comfortable shoes."

"Where are we going?"

"It's a surprise. See you in half an hour. Think you can be ready on time?"

"No problem."

She was ready on time, but just barely. She was wearing her favorite pair of stretch jeans, the ones she'd briefly wished she could have worn for him in St. Louis. They fit her like a glove, yet were surprisingly comfortable—and quite well worn. Despite what others might think, she didn't live in business suits *all* the time. The red-and-white striped rugby shirt she wore with them was a newer acquisition. On her feet were gym shoes, not as wild as Adam's, just a pair of white Keds. She'd brushed her hair away from her face and tied it back with a red scarf. All in all she thought she looked pretty casual.

Adam arrived right on time. The first thing he said was, "You should wear jeans more often."

The appreciative look he was giving her made her smile. "They're not exactly suitable at the office."

"That's a shame."

"Would you like to come in for a minute?" She nervously backed into her living room.

He looked around and raised an eyebrow at the sparse furnishings—two armchairs and a coffee table. "I see you've decorated the place in the minimalist style."

"I haven't had time to get much furniture yet," she said defensively.

"How long have you been living here?"

"Two years."

"I guess time flies by when you're having fun. And speaking of fun, I think you're going to enjoy what I've got planned for tonight. Are you ready to go?"

She nodded and followed Adam out to his car, a silvery-gray sports model. He held the door for her, then walked around to the driver's side. "Now will you tell me where we're going?" she asked, when he was seated beside her.

"To the lakefront. It's Venetian Nights tonight. You know, the parade of boats and the huge fireworks."

"It looks like it's going to rain."

It did rain, right after they'd reached the lakefront and set out the deck chairs that Adam had brought along. Luckily he'd also brought along a huge umbrella and a plastic raincoat. Julia thought he'd give her either the umbrella or the raincoat and keep the other for himself, but Adam decided that they'd share both. He bundled her into half the raincoat and held the umbrella over both their heads.

"Isn't this fun?" he asked as he pulled her closer to his side, tucking one end of the raincoat around her shoulder.

To her surprise it *was* fun. Adam made it so. He turned what could have been a dampening experience into something special. The wet weather didn't bother him one bit. He pointed out things she'd never have appreciated on her own—the sheets of rain hitting the lake water, the family that put a plastic tablecloth over their heads, the wild bobbing of the docked boats.

The sudden downpour had brought gusts of wind with it, but Julia felt dry and protected as she sat there huddled next to Adam. She also felt warm and captivated. She could smell the tanginess of the soap he'd used. She liked it. He'd shaved before he'd picked her up. She was tempted to run her hand along the line of his jaw and test the smoothness of his skin personally.

She had one arm around his waist, under the raincoat that covered them both. She wasn't sure where to put her other hand—on his knee, on his thigh? No, too tempting. On her knee? Too stiff. On the umbrella? He was already holding that and didn't seem to need any help. In the end she put her hand on his shoulder, holding the raincoat the way he was holding it on her shoulder. Her movement completed the circle.

"This is nice, huh?" he said with a grin.

She nodded and returned his grin. There was something about sitting in the rain that removed pretentiousness.

"Is this another of Mad Mac's barrier-breaking exercises?" she inquired lightly.

"Even *I* can't order rain to fall on request, but you have to admit, it's hard to keep your distance in a situation like this."

She didn't even want to keep her distance. He was definitely getting to her; there was no doubt about that.

She refocused her thoughts on their surroundings—their very wet surroundings. "Adam, I think they're going to have to cancel the festivities tonight."

"Oh ye of little faith. The rain will stop. Just wait and see."

He was right, as usual. The rain stopped in time for them to enjoy the cold fried chicken and coleslaw he'd brought along for their dinner.

"Here, have a bite of this drumstick." He held it up to her lips.

"I already have a piece of chicken."

"But not *this* piece. This piece is special."

She took a delicate nibble.

"It's good," she said, because he was looking at her so expectantly. "But what's so special about it?"

"Sharing it with you."

How was she supposed to keep her equilibrium when he said things like that to her? How was she supposed to guard her heart? It was difficult, very difficult. It would be so easy to give in to him. She had to monitor herself, make sure she didn't give too much too soon. She'd take this thing, whatever *this thing* between them was, very slowly; and perhaps that way she could avoid going overboard.

After dinner, after the sun had sunk behind the tall buildings behind them, Julia sat beside Adam and joined his cheering as the brightly decorated yachts of the Chicago Yacht Club went by—floats in a water-bound parade. A popular local TV news anchorman emceed the event, which was all in the name of charity. And afterward came the fireworks, set off over the lake.

When the first blast went off, Julia actually got goose bumps. The colorful explosion seemed to fill the entire sky as it rained red, white, and blue fire. The booming noise reverberated off the buildings behind them, on the other side of Grant Park. The echo was so deep she could feel it as well as hear it. More fireworks followed.

The display, which was synchronized to music, was the best that Julia had ever seen. Not that she'd actually seen many fireworks displays lately. It had to have been almost twenty years since she'd attended anything like this. She hadn't even been this excited about them as a child. But then she'd always felt like an adult, even when she'd only been five. The situation had demanded it.

Voices from the past floated through her mind. *"Don't cry anymore, Mommy. It'll be okay. I'll take care of you. I don't mind that we don't have a Christmas tree, really I don't. Here, you can have my ice cream. Want to hug my teddy bear? Want to hear a funny joke? Can't I help make you feel better?"*

"No," was the response she'd gotten over and over again.

As another chromatic explosion filled the sky, Julia deliberately pushed her thoughts aside and refocused all her attention on the fireworks display. It was much more enjoyable than thinking about her past.

"Well? What did you think?" Adam asked her when it was all over.

"It was fantastic! Thank you for bringing me. Having the fireworks over the lake like that really made them even more impressive."

"Have you ever been out on the lake?" he asked.

"On a boat you mean?"

"That's usually the safest way to be in the middle of the lake, yes."

"With you I can never be sure."

"Yes, you can. With me you can be very sure." Left un-spoken was the message that she could be sure he wanted her, and that he'd have her, sooner or later.

The message may have been unspoken, but it was com-municated very effectively in the heated look he gave her.

"No." She nervously looked away. "No, I've never been out on the lake." *And I've never been so deeply affected by a man before, either.*

"So how'd you like to go on a romantic dinner cruise next Friday? We're talking a bona fide romantic evening here— a suit for me, a filmy dress for you. Champagne, dancing under the stars, the whole enchilada. What do you say?"

"Yes."

His eyes widened in surprise. "What, no more argu-ments, no more persuasion needed? Just yes?"

"Yes."

"This is a first."

"Enjoy it while you can," she told him.

"I intend to." He kissed her.

The kiss may not have lasted long, after all they *were* surrounded by hundreds of people leaving the lakefront, but it was tender, and it was his way of telling her that he wanted her.

Afterward Julia's smile told him that his message had been received loud and clear. *Not a bad beginning for a first date,* he thought with a grin.

Julia had to work on Saturday, but they saw each other again on Sunday. Adam had invited her to brunch, but had omitted telling her that it would be at his sister's house. Ju-lia was not pleased by the news.

"You should have told me we were going to your sister's house," she said.

"Why? So you could have made an excuse not to come?"

"I don't like tricks, Adam. And I'm not wild about sur-prises, either."

"You enjoyed Friday night well enough, and that was a surprise. Come on," he coaxed her, "look at it this way. This will be your chance to give my family the third degree and ferret out all my childhood secrets. Don't you want to know what makes me tick?"

"No."

"May Ling will be there. You already met her and liked her, remember?"

Julia remained silent.

He sighed. "You're being difficult about this. Why?"

"I told you when we were in Boston. I don't get along well with families."

"With your family."

"With families, period."

"You haven't even met my family yet."

"That doesn't matter. I feel out of place at family functions. My family, or someone else's—it doesn't matter. There's just a certain inherent togetherness at these occasions that makes me feel..." She paused, uncomfortable with what she was about to disclose.

"Makes you feel what?"

She shrugged. "Left out, I guess."

"My family doesn't let anyone feel left out. House rule."

"Forced inclusion is just as bad."

He gave her an exasperated look. "Would you just relax? You might actually find that you enjoy yourself. They're just people. Forget they're even related to me. Just consider them to be six individual people."

"There will be six people there?"

Adam nodded. "More if you count all the kids."

Seeing her haunted expression, he felt guilty springing this on her. He'd been so excited about having her meet his family that he hadn't considered it from her point of view.

"Look, we'll only stay an hour. If you're still feeling uncomfortable, then we'll leave," he promised her. "No big deal."

"Oh, right. We'll just eat and run. That'll make a good impression, I'm sure."

"Stop worrying about impressions, about pleasing other people. How about pleasing yourself for a change?"

"If I wanted to please myself," she muttered, "we'd turn around and go home."

"If that's really what you want to do, then we'll do it. I can always call my sister and cancel."

Seeing that he was perfectly serious, she shook her head. "No, you can't do that. You accepted the invitation; you should attend. Just don't ever pull something like this again."

"I didn't realize it would upset you so much."

"I'm just nervous, I guess."

"What? You? The woman who can cope with anything? Listen, if you can deal with me, and you can, then my family is child's play."

"Easy for you to say. You know them."

"And you'll get to know them, too."

She sighed. "Do you always get your way?"

"I haven't gotten my way with you. Not yet, anyway. I live in hope, however."

His grin was too endearing for her to resist. Even though she smiled in return, she added a warning. "Just don't dump me in the kitchen with all the women while you men go off and watch a football game or some such thing."

"Hey, in my sister's household, it's the *men* who are stuck in the kitchen, and the *women* who watch the football."

"Really? That sounds interesting."

"See, I told you you'd have a good time."

And she did. Adam's family didn't fuss over her; they just accepted her. And she didn't think she'd ever be able to view football quite the same way again after hearing Adam's older sister Coleen talking about "tight ends."

His parents were obviously warm and demonstrative people. Before they'd left, they'd hugged Adam, who'd returned their embrace with a naturalness that Julia envied. The display of affection wasn't false or smothering. It was just...nice. Kind of like a Norman Rockwell scene. Kind of like the close-knit family she'd always wanted to be part of as a child.

"See, that wasn't so bad, was it?" Adam asked as they drove back to her apartment.

"They're nice people."

"Of course they are. After all, they *are* related to me."

"I know. Amazing how they've overcome that handicap, isn't it?" she retorted with a grin.

What was really amazing, Adam thought to himself, was the way Julia made him feel. Did she have any idea what that sassy smile of hers did to him? He wanted her so much he ached. He was trying to be patient, but he didn't know how much longer her could wait to make her his.

The next week was a long one for both of them. On Wednesday, Julia was unexpectedly sent to Detroit to do a series of seminars there. Adam stayed at home and waited for her calls. He was a man of action, and all this waiting was beginning to wear pretty thin. His phone conversations with her only served to remind him of how much he missed her, how much he wanted her, how much he wished she were there with him now.

It wasn't that he didn't have plenty of other things to keep him occupied—he did. Fall semester was starting in less than two weeks, and he still hadn't finished preparing his notes for the new class he was teaching—"Mastering Creativity." He'd much rather master Julia.

Friday finally arrived, and not a moment too soon as far as Adam was concerned. When he'd talked to Julia last night she'd sounded tired, but at least she was back in Chicago. And she was looking forward to their date; she'd told him so in a soft voice that had been more seductive than she knew, he was sure.

Now he stood outside her front door, waiting for her to let him in—into her apartment, into her life, into her bedroom and into her arms.

Julia jumped as the doorbell rang again. She'd just shimmied into her bronze silk dress, and she had to make sure she was adequately covered before going to answer the door. She checked the mirror in the hallway. Yes, everything was where it should be. The dress's neckline was seductive without being too obvious. And the dress did fit as if it had been made for her. The gold necklace and earrings she wore completed the outfit. She still had to find her shoes, however. But first she had to let Adam in.

"What took you so...long?" The last word was drawn out as Adam got his first good look at her. "You look fantastic!"

"Thanks," she said nervously. "I'm not quite ready yet, though."

"No? You look ready to me." I know I sure am, he thought to himself.

"I'm not wearing any shoes," she pointed out.

"Oh." He was more interested in her legs than in her lack of footwear.

"I was just about to look for them when you rang the bell."

"Want me to help you look?" he offered.

"No, thanks. They're probably under the bed."

"All the more reason for me to help you."

She put her hand on his chest, effectively stopping him in his tracks. "All the more reason for you to stay in the living room. Go try out my new couch."

"When did you have time to buy that?"

"I saw it a while ago and have been meaning to get it. I just didn't get around to it before."

As he settled onto the couch, she had to admit that he looked good in her living room. True to his word, he was wearing a suit along with his favorite hula-dancer tie. His blue shirt matched the blue of his eyes. Yes, he certainly did look great, but more than that, he fit in; he belonged. She shook her head and issued a silent warning to herself. Men like Adam didn't belong to anyone but themselves.

"Stop making such a big deal over nothing and find your shoes," she muttered to herself.

"Did you say something?" Adam asked.

"I said I'll be out in a minute."

"Don't take too much longer than that. We don't want to miss the boat."

They made it to Navy Pier with little time to spare. In fact, the ship was already boarding.

"It doesn't seem very crowded," she noted. "What did you do, reserve the entire ship?"

"A clever idea, but beyond my budget unfortunately. I don't know why it isn't crowded, but I'm not complaining."

"I wasn't complaining, either," she hurriedly clarified.

"Good." He took her hand in his. "Because tonight is going to be perfect."

"It is?"

"You don't sound very convinced," he noted. "Having second thoughts?"

"About what?" she asked cautiously.

"Going on this cruise."

"No, no second thoughts." Not about the cruise, anyway, she silently added. She still had plenty of second thoughts about the wisdom of getting involved with Adam.

Before Adam could question her further, they were welcomed aboard by a uniformed purser who was waiting to greet them at the end of the gangplank.

"Not many passengers tonight," Adam commented.

The purser shrugged. "I guess the weather is keeping some folks away."

"What's wrong with the weather?" Julia immediately asked.

"There's a severe thunderstorm warning out," the purser said, "but it's nothing to worry about."

"Nothing to worry about?" Julia repeated after they'd been shown to their window-side table. "Adam, I can't swim."

"Neither can I," he replied. "What's that got to do with anything?"

"What if the boat capsizes?"

"It's a ship," he corrected her, "and it's not going to capsize. We're not talking about a little motorboat here. This thing is huge. Look, the sign over there says it can carry over three hundred people."

"Most of whom stayed home tonight because of the weather."

"If it will make you feel better, we can go upstairs to the observation deck and take a firsthand look at the weather."

The ship's bouncing movement made Julia grateful for Adam's hand on her back as they walked up the steps to the higher deck. Unfortunately the view from the observation deck did not reassure Julia. A threatening mass of storm clouds was slowly rolling toward them from the west, beyond the city's skyline.

"You remember asking me a few minutes ago if I was having second thoughts about this cruise?" she inquired. "The answer is yes."

"Too late. We're already underway. Relax," he murmured as Julia tightened her death grip on the ship's railing. Putting his hands on her waist, he turned her to face him. "Look at it this way—the storm will add a little excitement to the trip."

"I don't need any more excitement." She put her hands on his shoulders. "You generate quite enough on your own, thank you."

"I do?"

She nodded. Their eyes met, and a moment later their lips did, too. Adam kissed her with hungry passion until the shrill sound of the ship's whistle startled them both, ending their embrace.

"We'll finish this later," he promised her huskily. "We've got all night."

Julia wondered what exactly he meant by *all* night, but felt awkward questioning him.

His next comment was prosaic enough. "Come on, let's go eat."

The ride was fairly smooth as they made their way around the buffet table on the enclosed lower deck. Aside from the usual entrée selections of roast beef and chicken, there was shark in teriyaki sauce, which Julia found to be surprisingly tasty. Somehow it seemed appropriate to be sitting there eating shark with Adam—a man who was something of a shark himself—while waiting for a storm to hit.

She couldn't help getting the feeling that Adam had set a hidden agenda for this evening. What was he thinking of as he sat there looking at her? Was he wondering, as she was, where the evening was going to end, what it was all leading up to? No, he wasn't looking at her as if he were a man who was *wondering*; he was eyeing her as if he were a man who *knew*.

"I'd like to propose a toast." He lifted his wineglass and gently clinked it against hers. "To us. Tonight is ours. Here's to spending every minute of it together."

As their eyes met over their wineglasses, Julia had no trouble translating the message in his eyes. It was suddenly clear to her that Adam believed the steamy looks were leading to one conclusion—her in bed with him. Tonight.

He certainly was taking an awful lot for granted, she decided testily. Feeling restless and strangely on edge, she looked away. All she'd agreed to was dinner. She wasn't ready for more yet. What happened to their agreement to date for a while? One week—two dates and a family brunch—that was it?

What more do you want? she asked herself. Time? Love? Safety? Security? A guarantee that you wouldn't repeat past mistakes? She wanted all that. And she wanted Adam.

As a clap of thunder warned of the approaching storm, Julia noticed that the ride was getting choppier. She could see whitecaps out on the lake as the wind picked up. The turbulence reflected her own feelings.

Julia knew it was a scientific fact that when a cold front met a warm front, a storm was born. She was also learning that as the cool front of her own emotions—her rational and in-control self—came up against the warm front—the passionate, giving side of her nature—a storm was taking place within her. Lightning crackled along her nerve endings, and her heart echoed the rumbling thunder. She felt hot and cold, changeable, volatile. Her inner tension kept building. The elemental power of the thunderstorm was only increasing the stormy state of her own conflicting emotions.

The explosion came later, after the cruise—at her apartment. Adam had come up with her, but when he'd kissed her, she'd been cool.

"What's wrong?" he asked.

"Nothing. I'm just tired. It's been a long day."

Normally Adam would have accepted her explanation, but tonight he wanted the truth from her, and he knew he wasn't getting it.

"Something else is wrong," he said. "You're pulling away from me, and I want to know why."

"What were you expecting?" she demanded crossly. "That I'd fall into bed with you? One romantic evening and *bingo*—" she snapped her fingers "—we'll make love? It takes more than that."

"I know what it takes," he retorted. "It takes this." He pulled her into his arms and lowered his lips to capture hers.

His kiss was like a match to dry kindling. She went up in flames, and so did her arguments, her second thoughts, her reservations. They might reappear later, but for now there was nothing but Adam. He consumed her, satisfying her aching need as only he could.

They were locked in each other's arms. Her hunger matched his as they kissed. Neither expected their emotions to get out of hand so quickly. It was as if they'd already waited decades for this moment and couldn't possibly delay the inevitable outcome a second longer.

Each kiss became more intimate than the last. Julia welcomed his passion and returned it with equal fervor. She could feel the warmth of his skin beneath his shirt, but it wasn't enough. She wanted to feel that skin beneath her hands.

Adam kissed his way from her mouth to the hollow at the base of her neck. He pulled her even closer, caressing the curves so delectably covered by the bronze silk dress. When he lifted his hands to her breasts, Julia shivered with pleasure. His lips captured her sighs, muffling them with a kiss that was heated and raw with need. Tongue met tongue in a slick interplay that erotically mimicked a more intimate joining.

With a tremendous amount of willpower, Adam broke away long enough to mutter against her ear, "If you have any second thoughts, you'd better say so now. Should I stay or leave?"

"Stay."

Eight

There were no more words spoken after that. All their attention was centered on getting to the bedroom as soon as possible. Even so, the trip was too far to go without a kiss or two—heated exchanges that held the promise of what was yet to come.

When they reached the bedroom, Adam proved more than capable of removing Julia's dress without removing his arms from around her. Julia, too, was able to continue kissing Adam even as she tugged his tie open and unbuttoned his shirt. The physical contact was never broken off for a moment. It was as if their passion had reached such a high level that nothing could stop it now.

Not that Julia wanted to stop. The thought didn't enter her mind. Nor did any other thought for that matter. She just wanted this pleasure to continue, wanted the hungry ache deep within her to be filled by Adam. He alone could satisfy the need growing inside her.

She removed his tie and shirt and tossed them onto a nearby chair with little concern for neatness. Now she was free to explore the bare expanse of his chest, the same way he was exploring the curves of her breasts. She touched him, marveling at the wonderful structure of the male body. Not just any male body—his. It was special. He was special.

She felt his heart pounding beneath the palm of her hand, a heart that increased its beat as her other hand lowered to undo his belt. She paused as Adam removed her bra and began touching her—slowly, seductively, heatedly. The sight of his tanned hand on her pale skin made her shiver. She felt as if he were branding her with his touch, marking her as his.

She wanted to do the same to him. The primitive need to possess flamed as brightly in her as it did in him. She arched against him, tightening her grip on his shoulder, pulling him closer.

He responded by taking the rosy crest of her breast into his mouth. The tugging action of his lips, the seductive swirl of his tongue made her knees weak. She couldn't take much more of this. The pleasure was so intense it was almost painful. And all the while, the aching need kept growing.

Her fingers trembled, but she managed to undo the zipper of his slacks.

He trembled as her hands brushed against him, intimately, wondrously. Each inch the zipper was lowered proved to be a delicious torture to him.

Cursing her awkward fingers, Julia worried that she was causing him pain when she wanted to bring him pleasure. She wished she were more experienced at acting the seductress and removing a man's clothing. When he groaned, her fingers stilled.

"No, it's okay," he said in a husky growl. "It's wonderful. You're wonderful." He took her hand in his and pressed it against him once more. "Keep going. Don't stop."

She couldn't stop, and neither could he. It was too late for that.

Soon afterward his slacks fell to the floor where he impatiently kicked them away.

Julia gave a startled gasp as he swung her into his arms and carried her the last few feet to the bed. She kicked her shoes off, which left her wearing only a pair of panties, a garter belt, and stockings. Adam lowered her to the bed with tender care. She pulled him down beside her, wanting to feel his warmth against her. He covered her like a blanket.

"I'm too heavy for you," he protested.

She shook her head. "No, you're just right."

"*We're* just right." He shifted against her, letting her feel the strength of his arousal. Meanwhile his hand was sliding up her thigh, skillfully and efficiently undoing her stocking and slipping it off. He'd just removed the second stocking when he growled with pleasure as she slid her hands beneath the waistband of his briefs.

Distracted, he kissed her with raw passion, his tongue emulating the thrusting motion of his body. "Oh, honey, feel what you do to me. I can't wait much longer. Are you protected?" The question was murmured into her ear.

Protected. Planned. Anticipated. She shook her head. She hadn't planned for this to happen.

"It's okay. I've got something." He moved away from her to reach for his slacks, which were still on the floor. He removed a packet from his pocket.

"So you did come prepared," she said, irritated by the reminder that he'd anticipated ending up in her bed.

He set the foil packet on the bedside table. "You don't sound very pleased."

"You seem very much in control of everything."

He returned her hands to his body. "Does that feel like I'm in control? I'm shaking like a teenager. I want you so much I can't think straight."

She restlessly shook her head. "I can't think at all."

"Good. You don't have to think, just feel."

He slid the panties from her. Now nothing separated them. Nothing interfered with their pleasure. And he did pleasure her, intimately stroking her with his fingers, lifting her to higher and higher plateaus of excitement. One final brush of his thumb, and she shattered into a million pieces, the pulses of ecstasy rippling through her.

Before she could fully recover, he rolled away from her for a moment. She eagerly welcomed his return.

A moment later she had him where she wanted him, deep within her. He filled her with glorious precision, making sure she could accept all he had to offer. She tightened around him, seductively welcoming him.

"Keep doing that, and this will be over before it's begun," he growled.

"Don't you like it?" she murmured.

"Too much." He rocked against her. "God, that feels so good. You feel so good."

"So do you," she whispered.

He moved again, setting the tempo—slowly at first but then faster, harder.

For Julia the pleasure built once more. She was wild with desire. The tension was tightening like a silken rope bringing them together.

Feeling himself about to lose control, Adam tried to slow down. Wanting to prolong the moment, he rolled onto his back, taking her with him.

She settled into her new position with feminine glory. She pressed her bent knees against his hips as he guided her with his hands. Her body recognized the rhythmic rise and fall. Her eyes were closed, her breathing reduced to sexy gasps of pleasure.

Watching her gave Adam great satisfaction, but not as great as the satisfaction he felt when she opened her eyes and smiled down at him. Bracing her hands on his shoulders she leaned forward and kissed him so passionately that it was an act of love in itself. Her forward motion increased the joyful sensation of their union, triggering the beginning of the end.

Adam felt the delicate shudders rippling through her and knew he was lost. With a muffled shout of triumph, he lifted her upward for one final thrust and then brought her down again, burying himself deep within her, wanting to become one with her soul as well as her body—and succeeding. They climaxed together, the pulsing waves of sheer ecstasy traveling from her body to his. They shared equally in the joy and the satisfaction as the contractions continued on and on.

Much, much later Adam gave her a supremely contented smile and murmured, ''I didn't think it was possible to feel that good and still live to talk about it.''

''Me, either,'' she whispered on the edge of a yawn.

Threading his fingers through her tousled hair, he guided her head onto his shoulder. ''Go to sleep,'' he said softly.

But, even though she was tired, she was too tense to sleep. Her earlier uneasiness was beginning to return. She'd definitely gone off the deep end this time. She'd been so determined to stay in control and look what had happened. He kissed her, and she went up in flames. Sure it had been wonderful, but now that she had time to reflect on it, her wildness and uncontrollable passion frightened her.

Abruptly sitting up, she held the covers up to her chin and reached over for her robe, which lay on a nearby chair. Despite what had just happened between them, or perhaps because of it, she felt particularly vulnerable.

''You don't need to wear a robe in front of me,'' Adam murmured.

''Yes, I do.''

He looked at her in amazement and amusement. ''Don't tell me you're shy after what we just shared.''

"Yes, I am shy." Julia was already feeling very jumpy, and his challenging her on this small point didn't ease that tension any. "Why are you making such a big deal out of my wearing a robe?"

"It's just that the way you fastened it around yourself reminded me more of a warrior preparing himself for battle than a woman putting on a simple piece of clothing. Are you trying to put up the fence again, mend the broken barriers? Why not just let yourself be yourself for a change? Relax. Kick back. You need to learn how to unwind."

"Would you stop trying to change me into something I'm not."

He frowned in confusion. "What's that supposed to mean?"

"You don't know me as well as you think you do. Sometimes *I* don't know *myself* as well as I think I do," she muttered as she began pacing the bedroom floor. "I didn't mean for this—for us—to happen this fast."

"Fast? Julia, we've known each other almost two months."

"Which isn't all that long. You make it sound like forever."

"Well, you made it sound like two hours. This wasn't just a quick roll in the hay, you know."

She stopped and looked at him. "Oh? And how am I supposed to know that?"

"Because you mean more to me than that. Don't you know that by now?" he asked with tender exasperation. "Haven't I shown you how I feel about you?"

She nodded. "You wanted me."

"I still want you; I'm bordering on needing you, and I've already fallen in love with you. Is that what you were waiting to hear?"

"There's no need for you to say that just because it's what you think I want to hear."

He glared at her. "Lady, you drive me crazy sometimes, do you know that? First you say you want me to tell you how I feel, and then when I do, you don't believe me. I can't win for losing here."

"Just tell me the truth."

"I already told you the truth. I'm not in the habit of lying."

She sighed. "Now you're upset."

"Hell, yes, I'm upset. Wouldn't you be if I called you a liar?"

"I didn't mean it like that," she said. "I meant that you didn't have to sugarcoat reality for me. I'm a big girl; I can take it."

"You're not only a big girl, you're a very sexy lady. I'm even turned on by the way you blush."

She put a hand to her flushed face and grumbled, "Before I met you, I hadn't blushed since I was a teenager."

"Then we're even, because before I met you I hadn't felt this . . . aroused . . . since I was a teenager."

"I know, the chemistry between us is incredibly strong."

"It isn't just chemistry; it isn't just attraction. Didn't you hear what I said earlier? I've fallen in love with you."

"Are you sure?" she asked hesitantly.

"What kind of question is that? Of course, I'm sure. What I'm not sure of is how you feel about me. Care to fill me in on that?"

She nervously fingered the belt on her robe. "It's not easy for me to put into words."

"You think it was easy for me? It was the pits. But those are the breaks. No pain, no gain."

She had to smile at his bluntly teasing assessment of the situation. "It shouldn't have to be this difficult, should it?" She took a deep breath. "All right. You already know that I wanted you, too, that I still want you. It's the loving and the needing part that has me scared to death."

"The fact that I feel that way about you, or that you feel that way about me?"

"Both."

"Not exactly the most passionate declaration of love, but I guess it'll have to do."

"I'm sorry," she said somewhat stiffly. "I'm not up-to-date on what to say in a situation like this."

"You could try saying that you enjoyed what we just shared, that you'd like to do it again real soon. Or how about throwing yourself into my arms and saying you adore me? That would be nice, too," he said wistfully.

She couldn't resist. She launched herself at him and kissed him. "I adore you!"

"No, don't say it if you don't mean it," he declared with noble stoicism.

She gave him a gentle sock in the arm for teasing her. "Stop making fun of me."

"Humor helps."

"I know it does. And I appreciate your trying to make things easier for me. I don't mean to be so contradictory. But frankly tonight threw me. I kissed you, and my control went right out the window."

"And you don't feel very comfortable being out of control, do you?"

"No."

"Does it help to know that I was out of control, too?"

"But you were prepared...."

"Prepared to protect you, but not prepared for the intensity of what we had together. I didn't plan for this to happen any more than you did. Well, maybe a little more than you did," he admitted with a rueful smile. "But we're both struggling to get used to these feelings. Give it some time and some more practice, and there's no telling where we might end up."

"We'd end up in bed again."

"We still are in bed," he pointed out.

"So we are." Her fingers tiptoed down his chest. "Seems a shame to just be talking when we could be practicing."

"A woman after my own heart."

"And after your body," she added with a seductive grin.

"That, too. So what are we waiting for?" He pulled her into his arms and rolled over so that he was leaning over her. "Let's start practicing. Who knows? You may yet get used to saying you love me. You might even learn to like it."

Yes, Julia thought to herself, but will I learn not to be afraid of it?

The answer to that question was slow in coming. As their relationship progressed at a steadier pace, Julia began to relax a little more and enjoy herself. She also enjoyed Adam. He made her laugh...he made her smile...he made her shiver...he made her ache, and then he made her melt with joy. He made her love him a little more each day.

He told her she should trust her instincts more. She told him he should be more logical. And they both told each other that they were loved, if not with words, then by their actions.

The week flew by. Adam started the fall semester of school; Julia was still waiting to hear about a possible promotion. Summer had turned into autumn which turned into the advent of the holiday season.

"What do you mean, you don't have a Christmas tree at your place?" Adam demanded as they lay cuddled together in bed early one Saturday morning. They were at his loft. "It's the first weekend of December already. You've got to get moving here."

"I don't want to move," she mumbled against his shoulder. "I'm comfortable right where I am. And I don't have a tree because it's against my lease. Live Christmas trees are a fire hazard."

"Don't you even have one of those artificial things?"

She nodded and stretched languidly. "I've got one in a box somewhere, but I haven't put it up."

"Tell you what, we'll go Christmas-tree shopping this morning. There's nothing in *my* lease about not having live trees."

"One of the advantages of living in a loft in a restored warehouse," she retorted. "This place is just about indestructible."

"I thought you liked it here."

"I do. It's very handy having all your living space in one large room this way. The round trip from the couch to the refrigerator to the bed is less than half of what it is at my apartment."

"Is that what you were counting last night? The number of steps it took us to reach my bed?"

"That's right. Why? What did you think I was doing?" she asked.

"Timing me," he promptly replied. "Giving me thirty seconds to get you to bed."

"You accomplished that in half that time."

"So I rushed you a bit. I slowed down once we reached the important bits, didn't I?"

She nodded and rubbed her bare foot down his leg. "You certainly did."

"Maybe we should put off our tree shopping until this afternoon," he murmured as he seductively caressed her.

"Maybe we should," she agreed and returned his caresses with a few of her own.

"How does this one look?" Adam asked as he held a hearty Scotch pine upright, knocking the base of the trunk against the frozen ground to get some of the snow off the branches.

Julia shook her head. "No, it's too lopsided."

"It's got character."

"It's missing half its branches. And, look, the needles are falling off."

"Yours would be too if you had to spend much time out here," Adam muttered. "It's freezing."

"Hey, shopping for a tree today was your idea not mine. Don't wimp out on me now."

"Me? Wimp out? Those are fighting words, lady." He grabbed her in one arm and kissed her cheek. "Mmm." He nuzzled his cold nose against her warm skin. "You smell good."

"It's eau de pine from that last tree I picked up."

"How many trees have we looked at now? At least fifty, I'll bet. And they've all been too lopsided, too short, too tall, too something."

"I'll know the right one when I see it. You told me that's the first rule of proper Christmas-tree shopping. To get the tree that really calls to you."

He released her and dropped the Scotch pine back onto the rejected pile. "I said that before I realized how picky you are. There's no such thing as a perfect tree, you know, not with a real tree anyway."

"I'm not looking for perfect."

"That's reassuring to hear," he noted dryly.

"Come on, there's only one more aisle to choose from."

As they walked the length of the final aisle, Adam was wondering if his toes were going to freeze inside his boots when he heard Julia exclaim, "There it is!"

"There what is?"

"Our tree."

He looked around. "Julia, there are about a hundred trees here. Care to be a little more specific?"

"That one over there, standing all by itself in the corner."

He looked at the tree and then back at her. "You're kidding, right?"

"No. It's perfect."

"Julia, the thing's got to be eight feet high if it's a foot."

"So what? You've got high ceilings in the loft."

"Its trunk is crooked."

"That gives it character." She tugged the tree upright for his appraisal. "Look how full the branches are."

"On that side, anyway."

"You only need them on one side. The other side will be against the wall. You said to get the one that called to me. Well, this is it. Can't you hear it? It's saying 'Take me home; take me home.'"

"I think the cold is getting to you."

"Don't you like it?" she asked uncertainly.

"It reminds me of Charlie Brown's tree. The one that no one else wanted, so he took it."

"I know. That's why I like it."

"It's why I like it, too," he admitted with a grin, before taking the evergreen from her hands. "Come on, tree. You've found yourself a home."

The next step was decorating it. Julia was accustomed to matching ornaments, usually color coordinated. One year her mother had decided to go all gold; the next year it had been green and red. And one year, the year her father walked out, there hadn't been a tree at all.

Adam didn't decorate like her mother at all. His decorations ranged from the sentimental to the absurd. They came in an assortment of colors, sizes and shapes. But each one had a personal meaning, and each one had a story.

She looked at the latest item in his hand and said, "You're not really going to put that thing on the tree, are you?"

"Sure I am. My nephew made it for me. It was the first thing he ever made for me. He must've been about two at the time. Pretty good for a two-year-old, huh? I tell you, creativity runs in my family."

"What's it supposed to be?"

"Santa Claus."

"Really? You could've fooled me. It looks more like a cookie."

"That was my second choice. Want to hand me one of those oatmeal cookies you made?"

She brought one over to him, but his hands were already full with a string of silver garland. "Open the hangar, here comes the plane," she teased him, making propeller noises as she aimed the cookie toward his mouth.

"You've been waiting ages to do that, haven't you?"

"That and a few other things."

"What?" he said with mock outrage. "Right here, under the Christmas tree?"

She looked startled. "No, I hadn't thought of that."

"Good thing I did, then."

"Mmm, good thing," she murmured as he kissed her.

They did have a good thing going. That Christmas was the best one Julia could ever remember having. It was certainly the most fun. She even seemed to be getting along better with her family. The only thing bothering her was the situation at work.

She expressed her concerns on New Year's Day—not to Adam, but to his turtle. Actually it was his nephew's turtle, and Adam had been sheltering it in his loft since Christmas.

"It's not that simple, Tut," Julia was telling the turtle. "I know, I know. You think I should just tell Helen that I'm not going to put in as much overtime as I used to, that I'd like to cut back on some of the traveling. But Helen is depending on me, Tut, and I can't let her down when she needs me. After all, she went out on a limb for me. She's the one who recommended me for the Intercorp project in the first place. I just have to hang on a little while longer, until I get that promotion she promised me. Once I become a project leader, there won't be as much traveling involved as there is now. I'd be doing more supervising, developing new courses, that sort of thing. Still it's true that I have cut back some of my hours, and sometimes I feel guilty about that. Okay, *frequently* I feel guilty about that. But look, I'm still putting in sixty-hour weeks. It's not as if I'm short-changing them, or have really slacked off. I'm still up to my eyeballs in work; I'm just not in over my head the way I used to be. There's no reason for me to feel guilty, right?'' She looked at the turtle and sighed. "So tell me, why do I feel this way?''

"Beats me," Adam said from the doorway, where he'd just walked in with a bag of groceries.

Startled, she whirled to face him. "How much did you hear?''

"Just you asking the turtle why you felt this way. What *way* is that?''

"Enamored of a man who not only talks to turtles but has me talking to them, too," she muttered as she put Tut back in his glass bowl.

"Hey, I told you that the turtle is just a device, a tool for expressing problems and verbalizing concerns.''

"Right. That's why you pick him up and rub him on his nose.''

"He gets lonely all alone in that glassy thing," Adam retorted. "He needs company.''

"Your nephew hasn't even broken it to your sister that he's gotten one turtle yet. I wouldn't go promoting the idea that he get another one.''

"Why not? Two can live as cheaply as one.''

Julia thought he was kidding. "Only if you're a turtle," she retorted. When he frowned, she wondered if he'd been talking about turtles after all.

"I can't understand what my sister has against turtles in the first place. She never did like them," he stated. "I can't imagine why.''

Julia relaxed. So he'd been frowning over his sister's aversion to turtles. Once again she'd worried, if only for a moment or two, over something that was meaningless. She had to break herself of this habit of overdramatizing things, of making mountains out of molehills. She had to lighten up, stop looking for hidden meanings. She also had to answer Adam. "I can understand your sister's feelings." It was her own feelings that Julia sometimes had trouble translating. "For one thing, turtles aren't exactly the most warm and cuddly of pets."

"If you want warm and cuddly, come to me." Adam slid his arms around her and nuzzled her ear. "If you want advice, check with the turtle. Tut did mention that you showed tremendously good judgment by becoming enamored of me, didn't he? You heard him, right?"

The only thing Julia could hear at the moment was the pounding of her heart. Adam had that effect on her, and time had only made it worse—or better—depending on one's perspective. Her own perspective was completely out of whack. When she was in his arms like this, she couldn't think of anything but him.

When she was with Adam everything seemed perfect, but when she was away from him, she'd worry about that perfection. There were even times when she was *with* him that she worried—about the pile of work left sitting unattended in her briefcase. Then there were all the times at work when she worried about not spending enough time with him.

Julia felt as if she were performing a juggling act using delicate hand-blown glass ornaments, trying to balance various fragile responsibilities without making any mistakes. One misjudged catch, and she'd end up with a shattered mess.

There was so much at stake. Helen was counting on her to do a good job. Adam was counting on her to be a good lover. And Julia was counting on herself not to let anyone down. But she was afraid that in trying to please everyone, she wasn't pleasing anyone at all.

Nine

Helen called Julia into her office the first workday after the New Year break. "We need to talk."

"If it's about the participant responses compilation, I'll have it ready this afternoon," Julia promised.

"No, it's not about that." Helen waited until Julia had come in and sat down before quietly saying, "It's about attitude. I've noticed a difference in yours over the past few months, and I think we should talk about it."

Julia's stomach plummeted to her toes. "I wasn't aware that there was any problem."

"I know, and that's part of what worries me. Julia, I don't have to tell you how demanding this job is, the number of hours required, the traveling away from home. It's not a job for everyone. Relationships have often had to suffer as a result of the high demands of this type of position. It's unfortunate, but it's a fact. And there's no getting around the fact that it's even more difficult for us as women. Men are able to depend on their wives to take care of so many things; their homes, their kids. But a woman has got to do those things in addition to getting the job done at work."

Julia shook her head in confusion. "I don't have any kids, or even a house for that matter."

"No, but you've got a relationship. It's Adam MacKenzie, isn't it?" Helen didn't even wait for a reply before shaking her head. "I should have seen this coming, I guess. I just never expected you to go off the deep end this way."

The accusation stung. "I haven't gone off the deep end," Julia protested. "If you've found fault with something I've done, with my work, I wish you'd be more specific and tell me."

"It's not your work per se; it's your attitude as I said earlier. How can I put this? It's not as..."

"Obsessive as it used to be?"

"Dedicated is the word I would have used. And this position requires absolute dedication." Helen's expression softened. "I'm only speaking to you as a concerned associate here. I want to see you get that promotion you've been working for. Don't slack off now, not when you're so close. I'd hate to see all your hard work go down the drain as a result of your distraction over a man. You've got to set priorities, Julia."

"Are you saying it's impossible for a woman to have a relationship—a private life and a professional one?"

"Not impossible, no. But in this case, with this particular position, it is improbable. There just aren't enough hours in the day. Haven't you discovered that yet?"

Julia looked away. "It's simply a matter of being organized," she stubbornly maintained.

"I don't think you can apply your efficiency techniques here, Julia. They won't work. There are choices you're going to have to make, choices that will be difficult, I'm sure. But they're choices that you can't put off much longer."

"I'm sorry if you feel that my work hasn't been up to par," Julia said stiffly. "I've tried very hard not to let my personal life interfere with business."

"You'll just have to try harder," Helen stated. "And here's your chance. I've got a rush project for you. It involves the Intercorp office down in New Orleans. The follow-up seminars we set up for this week are in trouble. Karl was supposed to fly down tomorrow, but he's in the hospital, with appendicitis of all things."

"Will he be all right?" Julia asked, immediately concerned.

"I presume so."

Julia made a mental note to send him a card and some flowers.

"Anyway," Helen continued, "we've substituted one of your seminars, the one on time management, for the presentation Karl was going to give. Your flight leaves tomorrow morning at 7:30. You'll be returning Saturday morning."

"Saturday morning?"

"Yes. Why? Do you have a problem with that?"

After the lecture Helen had just given her on team spirit and attitude, how could she say that Friday was her birthday and that Adam had planned a special evening for her. She couldn't. "No. There's no problem."

And there wasn't any problem, at least not an immediately apparent one. Adam was understanding when she explained the situation to him later that evening. But then Adam had never complained about the amount of time she had to spend working or about the frequent out-of-town trips she had to take.

At first she'd welcomed his understanding and appreciated it. Now she was beginning to wonder and to worry. Did he miss her while she was gone? Did he even notice, let alone mind that she was leaving? How could he really need her, love her, if he wasn't at all bothered by her absence? Didn't he care?

Granted, she didn't want a man who tied her to his side and wouldn't let her be her own person, but surely there had to be some kind of middle ground between total domination and complete indifference.

She didn't know. There were times, and this was certainly one of them, when this relationship stuff was impossible for her to figure out.

"We'll celebrate when you get back," Adam said. "Saturday, right?"

"Yes, I'll be back on Saturday, barring any complications. But then complications seem to be the norm today," she muttered darkly. "Why should things start going smoothly now?"

"What complications?" Adam questioned.

"Don't ask," she said, even though she wanted him to.

"Okay, I won't."

There it was again, she silently grumbled. His reluctance to communicate. Forget the fact that she'd been less than forthcoming herself. Adam didn't appear to care about her troubles. Or if he did, he wasn't relaying that fact to her. And it wasn't as if he were the strong, silent type, unable to express his feelings. Adam was usually an excellent communicator—it was part of his training, part of his teaching. It was part of her training and teaching, too, she reminded herself, but that didn't seem to be helping her any.

Julia left for New Orleans feeling restless and out of sorts. The first day's seminars were filled with technical glitches. The slide projector she'd requested hadn't shown up until the session was almost over. A number of handouts mysteriously disappeared, and five participants were late. Outwardly Julia was able to switch gears smoothly enough; indeed she used the incidents as an example of the need to be adaptable. But inside she was a mass of nerves. She didn't need anything else going wrong now. She already felt as if Helen had placed her on probation, demanding that she prove herself all over again. For Julia, it had become a matter of pride to show Helen that she was worthy.

When she finally returned to the hotel it was too late to call Adam, who had an early class in the morning. He hadn't tried calling her either; the message light on her phone wasn't lit.

The next day was almost a repeat of the previous one, only this time she returned to her room early enough to call Adam.

"How's it going?" he asked her cheerfully.

Julia thought that the least he could do was sound as if he was missing her. Then she quickly reprimanded herself for being contrary. She should be grateful that he wasn't making demands on her right now. Heaven knows she had her plate full as it was. "It's going okay."

"So, tomorrow's your birthday," he said.

"I know."

"No need to sound so glum about it. I sent you a present, you know. It's rather large. Maybe you should leave a message at the desk telling them to put it in your room when it arrives. I wouldn't want anything happening to it."

"You sent me a present?"

"Of course."

"I thought we were going to celebrate when I get back."

"We are. Now remember to tell the desk to expect a package from me and tell them to put it in your room."

"I will."

"Be sure and tell them my name," he reiterated. "I wouldn't want my package getting mixed up with the express mail going back and forth between you and your office."

"Right."

"Let me know how you like it."

"I will," she promised.

"Oh-oh, there's the doorbell. My pizza has arrived. I've gotta go. Talk to you soon."

Julia hung up, feeling morose. Apparently when it came to either talking to her or eating pizza there was no contest. The pizza won hands down.

She didn't know why she was feeling so sensitive. Maybe it was because of her birthday and the fact that she was leaving her twenties behind and entering her thirties. Or maybe it was because she was sitting all by herself in a hotel room in a strange city with nobody to talk to.

She'd been away on business on her birthday before. It never bothered her, but this year it did. She'd been telling the truth when she'd once told Adam that she usually ignored her birthday. But that had been before she'd met him. Now, after having celebrated Christmas with him—another special occasion she used to ignore—she wanted to regain some of the carefree magic he'd made her feel. She wanted to recapture that childlike feeling of wonder and excitement. She wanted to go home.

She thought of calling her mother but rejected the idea. She didn't want her mother hearing how depressed she was, and she was too tired to act cheerful. She even considered calling Patti but knew her younger half sister would first needle her about her age and then interrogate her about Adam. She didn't feel able to cope with that right now. And that disturbed her. Coping had always been her specialty, one she'd been very proud of. But lately it seemed to her that she hadn't been coping very well at all. The juggling act of responsibilities was getting harder and harder to perform.

Her mood didn't improve the next day. She returned to her hotel room that evening feeling decidedly depressed and unsettled. She missed Adam.

"Ms. Trent!" the concierge greeted her, loudly. Apparently she hadn't heard him the first time. "That package you were expecting arrived, and we put it in your room as you requested."

"Thanks."

For the first time all day, her spirits perked. She wondered what Adam could have gotten her that would be so large. With his talent for creativity, there was no telling what it might be. Her steps were lighter as she hurried to her room.

A colorful Happy Birthday sign had been draped across the outside of her doorway. Not knowing what to expect, she unlocked the door and opened it with some trepidation.

The first thing she noticed was the large box on the dresser. The second thing she noticed was that there was someone sleeping on her bed! Her startled gasp was prevented from turning into a full-fledged scream by the sudden realization that the someone on her bed was none other than Adam.

Delighted, she leaned down to kiss him.

"Mmm." He grabbed her and tugged her down onto the bed next to him. "You're late."

"What are you doing here?"

"Surprising you." He blinked at her sleepily. "Did I succeed?"

"Yes."

"Good," he said. "Then go back outside and come in again."

"What for?"

"You'll see."

When she made her second entrance into her room, Adam was ready for her. Shouting "Surprise!" he doused her with several handfuls of confetti.

"The maid is going to love you," Julia said in between her laughter.

"Forget about the maid. As long as *you* love me."

"I do." She threw her arms around him and hugged him tightly. "I'm so glad to see you."

"Maybe I should surprise you more often."

"You're always surprising me."

He tipped up her chin and kissed her again. "Come on, open your presents." Taking her by the hand, he led her over to the dresser.

"Presents?" she repeated. "I only see one."

"Never judge a present by it's cover," he advised her.

"I thought that saying only pertained to books."

"Shows what you know. Go on," he said. "Open it."

She unwrapped the large box only to find several smaller boxes tucked inside. The first one she opened had a tape of Tchaikovsky's 1812 Overture in it. She'd just reached for another present when there was a knock at the door.

"Ah, right on time," Adam noted appreciatively. "I told them to bring it ten minutes after you entered the lobby."

"Bring what?"

"Ta-dah!" He opened the door with a flourish and a waiter walked in with a silver tray. On it was the largest hot fudge sundae Julia had ever seen. Stuck into the whipped-cream topping were three candles, already lit.

Adam directed the waiter to put the tray on the table next to the presents. "Okay, now make a wish," he told Julia.

Julia wished she could always be as happy as she was at that very moment. And then she blew out all three candles.

After she and Adam shared the sundae there were more birthday presents to open. A lovely poster of a Monet painting, her own copy of the movie *Casablanca*. And then there was the exquisite pearl necklace he'd gotten her to match the pearl earrings he'd given her for Christmas.

"Oh, Adam." Overwhelmed, she ran a trembling finger along the pearls' shimmering surface. "You shouldn't have."

"Yes, I should. Here, allow me."

She held her hair out of the way as Adam helped her with the clasp of the necklace. She already wore the earrings.

"It's lovely," she whispered.

"So are you." He dropped a kiss on the bare nape of her neck before letting her hair cascade back down onto her shoulders. Standing behind her, he looked into the mirror they were both facing, willing her eyes to meet his. "When I got the set, I dreamed of seeing you wearing it and nothing else."

"You dreamed that?" She gave him a sultry smile and began slowly unbuttoning her blouse. "After you've gone through so much trouble to surprise me for my birthday, the least I can do is make your dream come true."

She satisfied that dream and several others as they made love with a slow passion that shattered their threshold of pleasure and took them to new heights of ecstasy.

The next morning Julia was dismayed to find she'd overslept. "I'm going to miss my flight," she exclaimed in a voice still husky with sleep. "I left a wake-up call for six. It's almost seven already. What happened?"

"I canceled it." Adam tugged her back into his arms. "And your ticket, too. Or rescheduled it to be more exact. We both return to Chicago Sunday evening. We have some unfinished business here." Seeing the gleam in her eyes, he said, "Not that kind of business."

"I didn't say a word," she said innocently.

"You didn't have to. The way you looked said it all."

She settled her head more comfortably on his shoulder. "What kind of unfinished business were you referring to then?"

"I seem to recall that the last time we were down here, we planned on going to visit a few plantations."

"You've got an incredible memory."

"Just one of my many talents," he modestly replied.

"I know." She ran her hand over his hip. "I know."

"You keep that up and we're not going to make the first plantation tour." He groaned as her hand slid lower. "Forget the plantations. I may keep you in bed the entire day!"

"Promises, promises."

It was almost noon before they did eventually leave the hotel and venture out in the car that Adam had rented. After visiting the lavishly restored San Francisco Plantation, they crossed the Mississippi River on a ferry boat and headed for their second stop—Oak Alley Plantation.

"This place looks familiar to me," Julia said as they drove down the entryway to the visitors' parking area at the back of the house. To her eyes it looked like something right out of *Gone with the Wind*, thanks in no small part to the huge live oak trees lined up in two evenly spaced rows. They were the loveliest trees Julia had ever seen. Even in January their leaves created a long verdant tunnel leading to the front of the plantation house.

"It's been used as the location for several TV movies," Adam replied. "The huge oaks in front are their trademark."

"They're beautiful." She looked down at the brochure she held in her hands, the one with the map she'd been using to guide them there. "It says here that the trees were planted sometime in the early 1700s, a hundred years before the present house was built. I'm glad they didn't knock them down to build the river levee the way they did at San Francisco Plantation. Trees like this can't ever be replaced."

Again they took a tour of the inside of the plantation house, but Julia was more fascinated by the exterior view than the interior decorations.

Adam noticed her preoccupation and offered to walk with her down the quarter-mile long "Oak Alley." He smiled when he caught Julia counting the trees as they went by.

"There are twenty-eight," she announced as they reached the gate at the front of the property. "Fourteen on each side."

"You like it here?"

"It's beautiful."

"Not too spooky for you?"

"Spooky?" she repeated.

"Didn't you notice those photographs in the entryway? The ones of the resident ghost, the legendary Lady in Black?"

"I must have missed that."

"She was standing looking out at these very trees. The photo was taken fairly recently, within the past few years. Makes you wonder, doesn't it?"

"Wonder what?"

"What it would be like to stay here, among other things."

"I don't know about ghosts, but it must be lovely here by moonlight."

"I'm glad you said that because I've made arrangements for us to spend the night in one of the cabins they rent out."

She looked at him in surprise. "You're kidding."

"Would I kid you?" he retorted.

"Yes, and you do constantly."

"This time I'm perfectly serious. Does staying here meet with your approval?"

She hugged him. "It sounds perfect."

He had high hopes that it would be. He had big plans for the evening and he didn't want anything going wrong.

"I feel like a cast member of *Les Misérables* in this outfit," Julia said a few hours later as she stepped out of their cabin's bathroom, dressed in a romantic, long, layered skirt and a white peasant blouse. Adam had found the outfit tucked in a corner of her closet and had brought it along with some other clothing he'd picked up from her apartment. "I feel silly." She turned around ready to return to the

bathroom and change into something more sensible, but
Adam put his hands on her shoulders and stopped her.

"You don't look silly." He ran a caressing finger across
the low, scooped neckline of her white blouse. "In fact, you
look incredibly sexy."

"I do?" She sounded doubtful even to her own ears.

"You do." Adam was emphatic. "With your hair all
loose like that you look kind of wild and wanton."

"That does it!" she exclaimed. "I'm not going out in
public in this outfit."

"Who said anything about going out in public?"

"I seem to recall you promising me dinner. I'm starv-
ing."

"Don't worry, you won't go hungry. I'll take care of all
your appetites." He trailed his hand down her arm, his fin-
gertips barely brushing her skin.

Julia felt the familiar heat stealing through her body and
into her heart. He had only to touch her, and she went up in
flames. The magic between them seemed to increase as time
went by, and her hopes for regaining control of her wild
emotions seemed to dwindle.

Adam lifted her hand to his lips, placed a kiss on her palm
and then closed her fingers around it. "I've ordered dinner
in our suite. They've already set it up in the front parlor."

He gallantly offered her his arm and escorted her from the
antique-filled bedroom to the equally antique-filled parlor.

"Candlelight? Nice touch," she said approvingly.

"I thought so." He pulled out the chair for her. "Your
seat, ma'am."

"Thank you, sir."

They dined on a selection of local seafood. It was delicious, but neither one of them was really paying that much
attention to the food. Adam was too distracted by the way
Julia's blouse hung on the verge of slipping off one shoulder. Julia was distracted by Adam's handsome dark looks,
which were made even more dramatic by the flickering

candlelight. With these surroundings it was easy to imagine that they'd stepped back in time. The billowy white shirt and pleated dark slacks Adam wore made him look like a nineteenth-century adventurer. Even his black suspenders fit into the fantasy. They were acting out their own version of *Gone with the Wind*, with her playing Scarlett to his Rhett.

The fantasy continued as they went for an after-dinner walk around the grounds. The full moon created a mystical light that seemed more suited to ghosts than to mere mortals. It felt as if they were surrounded by the past, as if it were a tangible presence.

The cool crisp temperatures eventually forced them back inside. Adam helped Julia remove her coat just as she helped him remove his. Afterward there was something sensually timeless about the way she went into his arms. Their kiss was equally eternal. Adam's lips were warm as he chased away the lingering chill and raised her temperature by at least a full degree.

But there was more to come. His hands slid from her waist down to the curve of her derriere where he gathered a handful of her ruffled skirt and drew her even closer. His fingers inched the material of her skirt upward until he reached the silky skin beneath. The things he did to her made her gasp with pleasure.

His knee nudged her shaky legs apart, and Julia sank against him, welcoming the support of his bracing thigh. Cupping her bottom in his hands, he lifted her up and let her slide back down against him. The ensuing friction made her aware of his arousal. Julia closed her eyes. Excitement washed over her as Adam's lips strayed from her mouth to her ear.

"Do you like this?" He lifted her again.

She nodded and tightened her grip on his shoulders as yet another wave of pleasure shook her.

"Do you want more?"

"I want you," she whispered huskily.

"You've got me."

"Not where I want you."

"Soon. But first..." He went on to whisper erotic promises of every single thing he wanted to do to her, with her, for her.

Eventually she stopped the provocative sound of his raspy voice by hungrily putting her lips over his.

The kiss intensified as Adam tasted her, savoring the warmth of her mouth. He growled his appreciation as her tongue boldly greeted his, exploring him as he was exploring her. His hands clenched, crushing her bunched-up skirt. The material was cool and crisp in his hands, but the woman beneath was fiery and soft. He loved the way her passion matched his, the way she was so wild and alive in his arms.

He'd never been so grateful that a bed was nearby. Otherwise he might have been tempted to take her right there where they stood. Instead he moved them both the few feet into the bedroom and fell onto the bed with her still in his arms.

He wasn't expecting the mattress to bounce as much as it did. Neither was Julia, and her startled gasp interrupted their kiss.

They looked at each other and laughed.

"I guess we're lucky the bed didn't break," he said.

"Hey—" she gently socked his arm "—I'm not that heavy."

"You may not be, but I sure am."

"Mmm." She ran her hands down his back, around his waist, over his stomach and lower—simply enjoying the freedom to touch him. He was heavy, warm, throbbing with need; and the knowledge that she was the reason gave her a wonderful sense of satisfaction. But not half of the satisfaction that was yet to come.

He kissed the huge smile from her lips and softly told her, "I love it when you touch me there."

"I love it when you touch me anywhere," she replied as he slid the peasant blouse from her shoulders.

"Why did you wear a bra under this?"

"To make your life complicated."

"Good thing I'm not a man who gives up easily." He slipped his index finger under the silky lingerie's front-opening clasp.

"You're not a man who gives up at all." She played along as he teasingly pretended to be unable to figure out how to remove a bra he'd been known to get rid of in two seconds flat in the past. "I'm sure you'll be able to figure it out."

Before he did, he figured out exactly where his touch gave her the most pleasure. The lingerie's silky sheerness only served to accentuate his caresses, adding another dimension of delight as his prowling fingers skimmed and stroked, rubbed and tickled, cuddled and massaged.

In the end Julia undid the bra herself, unable to resist the need to feel his hands on her. She also unbuttoned his shirt and tugged it down his arms, where it got caught on his wrists because she'd failed to unbutton the cuffs first.

While his hands were temporarily restrained, Adam allowed his lips to take over the seduction as he tasted her, delicately flicking his tongue along her breast from the creamy slopes to the rosy tips.

Distracted she abandoned her work on his shirt cuffs to slide her fingers through his dark hair and tug him closer. She could feel his cheek pressing against her breast as he nuzzled her, devilishly brushing his mouth back and forth.

She repaid his sensual teasing by moving against him, brushing her bare torso against his.

Suddenly he couldn't get rid of his shirt fast enough, or the rest of his clothes, either. Moments later her skirt joined the pile of discarded clothing. He slowed down briefly as he removed her silky panties. His fingers trembled as he ran his hand back up her thigh to explore her feminine secrets. When he found her—all sultry and slick, so obviously ready for him, his control nearly deserted him. It was all he could do to roll away and take care of protecting her before making their union complete.

"Now," Julia whispered with a provocative smile. "Now I've got you where I want you."

"And I've got you," Adam growled before swiftly covering her mouth with his own. The thrust of his tongue mimicked the thrust of his body as he took her with him, racing from one plateau of ecstasy to the next. The end came quickly and powerfully. With one final surge of motion he rushed them both over the top of the peak and sent them tumbling down the other side.

When Julia next opened her eyes, sunlight was streaming through the lace curtains and Adam was propped on one elbow, looking down at her.

She blinked at him sleepily. "What's wrong?"

"Nothing."

"Then why are you staring at me?"

He smiled at her. "I like staring at you."

"Couldn't you sleep?"

"I slept fine. I've just been waiting for you to wake up." He played with a lock of her hair. "You look so cute when you're asleep."

She wrinkled her nose at him.

"No, really you do," he said. "You sort of curl your hand under your chin like a little girl. Makes me kind of wonder what a little girl of yours, of ours, would look like. Makes me wonder why I haven't asked you to marry me before now. I love you, Julia. I want to marry you."

"Adam, it's too early in the morning to tease me."

"I'm perfectly serious. What do you think of a Valentine's Day wedding?"

She closed her eyes and muttered, "I must be dreaming."

"So you like the idea, too. Great! Valentine's Day it is."

Her eyes flew open again. "Adam, this isn't funny."

"I'm not trying to be funny. I'm trying to propose to you. So what's your answer—yes or no?"

For Julia the answer was sheer panic. *Now what are you going to do?* she asked herself. She didn't have an answer to that question either.

Ten

Julia stalled for time. "What was the question again?"

"I said I'm trying to propose to you. You know, propose—as in ask you to marry me."

"Oh."

"Oh?" he repeated teasingly. "That's all you've got to say? What kind of answer is that?"

"It wasn't an answer; it was a reaction."

"Not exactly the one I was hoping for," he retorted ruefully. "You don't have to look so surprised. Considering the fact that I love you and you love me, my proposing marriage isn't really that outlandish or radical, you know."

"It's just . . . I'm not ready for this," she whispered unsteadily.

"Too early in the morning for you?"

"Adam, I'm serious," she said almost desperately. "I mean I'm *really* not ready for this."

"Why are you making this so hard on me? It's a simple question. Will you marry me—yes or no?"

"It's not a simple question."

"Sure it is. What's so complicated about it?" he demanded.

"Everything."

"That tells me a lot."

"I told you I need more time." Julia tried to still the panic that had quickly taken hold once she'd realized that he was indeed serious. "We'll talk about it after I take a shower."

He clamped his hand around her arm, preventing her escape and keeping her by his side. His earlier teasing manner was replaced by an implacable stubbornness. "You're not going any place until you answer my question."

Feeling cornered, she resorted to sarcasm. "What are you doing? Making me an offer I'm not allowed to refuse?"

"Are you refusing it?"

She tugged her arm away from his restraining hold. "I'm saying, for about the tenth time, that I need more time to consider the matter."

"Until when? Until you've completed an efficiency report on the pros and cons of marriage versus those of staying single?"

"You're not taking this very well," she informed him.

"Excuse me if I get a little upset when the woman I love says she doesn't know whether or not she wants to marry me!"

"You're paraphrasing my words—and inaccurately, too."

"Then say what you mean," he said impatiently.

"I mean I'm not ready to get married. I need more time," she repeated yet again, as if it were her talisman.

"Time for what?" Anger crept into his voice. "I don't understand what the problem is."

"That's obvious," she shot back and then sighed. "I'm sorry. I didn't mean to snap at you. It's just that you've..."

"Caught you by surprise. Yes, I know. You've made that much very clear. You've surprised me too. I wasn't exactly expecting you to hem and haw this way."

"Hem and haw?"

"That's right. I asked you a direct question, and I'd like a direct answer."

"I can't give you one, Adam. It's a complicated issue."

"Try explaining it to me."

"I'm still trying to balance the relationship we already have. Marriage..." She paused and shook her head. "Marriage is another step entirely."

"Is it me, or is it marriage you're objecting to?"

Julia paused, searching for the right words to say that it was her, him, and marriage—the whole enchilada. She wasn't good enough at handling the romantic relationship they already had. She didn't have her act together enough to progress on to the next step yet.

But her silence was damning in Adam's eyes. "Forget it." He shoved back the covers and got out of bed. "Go take your shower and get dressed. It's a long drive back to New Orleans, and we've got a flight to catch."

"Wait a minute!" Now she was the one who reached out to grab his arm. "Don't you think we should talk about this?"

"Why bother?" He gave her such a cold look that she released her hold on him. "It seems to me that you've already made up your mind."

"Why are you acting this way? Are you angry because I asked you for more time?"

"I'm angry because you're stalling, putting up barriers again. I thought we'd progressed beyond that by now, but here you are, regressing back to type."

She took exception to his words. "Stop making me sound like some kind of emotional cripple."

"You said it. I didn't," he retorted nastily.

She replied in kind. "If this is the way you issue a proposal, I'm not surprised you haven't been married before!"

"I've never asked anyone before," he said quietly.

She was suddenly filled with remorse. "Oh, Adam. Why are we hurting each other this way? Come back to me so we can talk about this." When he made no move to join her, she said, "Look, at least let me try and explain my reasons to you. If you really loved me . . ."

Adam exploded. "What do you mean—*if?* After all I've said and done, you still have doubts? You still want me to prove myself, to prove my love for you? Is that what this demand for more time is? Another test? If so, you can forget it."

"I can't believe you're acting this way." She looked at him and shook her head in bewilderment.

"And what way is that? Like a man who's reached the end of his patience? I have. I've been patient and understanding long enough. I played the role of liberated and understanding lover. I tried not to be demanding, never complained about your long hours, pretended the trips didn't bother me. And where's it gotten me? No place. You're still stalling, putting up barriers like you have in the past. If that's the way you want it, fine. I'm going to take a shower." He stormed out of the room.

Julia sat in bed, listening to the roar of the shower and unable to believe that Adam had just walked away in the middle of their argument. She couldn't believe the argument, either. But the thing that upset her the most was his admission about playing the role of lover. He'd only been *pretending* to be understanding. If he'd pretended about that, what else had he been faking? She didn't doubt his love for her, but suddenly a whole new closet of worries was opening. What were his real feelings about relationships? These were things they should have been talking about and certainly needed to discuss before the subject of marriage was brought up.

She could see that; why couldn't he? And what had made him propose now? Why hadn't he given her some warning first, so she could have prepared herself for this eventuality. Why was he trying to complicate things now?

She shoved her hands through her hair, realizing that she was viewing this matter selfishly. She didn't imagine that Adam was feeling any better than she was. And he was as much in the dark about *her* worries and concerns as she'd been about *his* resentment against her long hours. He couldn't know what she was thinking or feeling, because she hadn't told him. He hadn't given her the chance.

But Julia was determined that she would make him listen. This was only a temporary impasse. They'd discuss things like the two reasonable adults they were and reach an understanding. They loved each other; they just had differing views on the advisability of marriage at this time. She put her robe on and sat there, mentally preparing her explanation.

But when Adam returned from the bathroom, fully dressed and utterly remote, he didn't look any more ready to listen than he had when he'd stomped out earlier.

"Adam . . ."

"I'll go load the car."

"Wait a minute." She jumped out of bed and grabbed the cuff of his trench coat, preventing him from putting it on. Under other circumstances she might have found her actions amusing; she was pretty sure Adam would have been amused. But now he was just plain irritated. "This is silly, Adam. We need to talk."

He gave her another cold look. "I think we've both said enough already."

"We've hurt each other enough," she agreed. "I don't want to do that. I love you, Adam."

"But you don't *want* to love me, do you? You don't have the time to love me. I get in the way, right? Distract you from your precious career."

"It's not the career, Adam. It's obligations. I had no idea that my traveling bothered you so much, or the long hours, either, for that matter. You never said a word. I'm not a mind reader, you know. I've got no way of knowing how you feel if you don't tell me."

"The same is true for me," he retorted. "I have no way of knowing how you feel if you don't tell me. Otherwise I just have to guess at your feelings based on your actions, on what you *do* tell me. And your actions and your words tell me that I'm not important in your life."

Her hand dropped to her side. "How can you say that after the way we made love last night? How can you say that it wasn't important?"

"How can *you* say it?" he countered.

"I haven't."

"Yes, you have."

"How? By saying I need more time to think about your proposal? I would have thought that the argument we're having right now is proof that I'm right, that we both need more time to think about this. We've obviously been talking at cross-purposes here. There are unresolved issues and misunderstandings that need to be cleared up."

"Always so logical, aren't you?"

His sarcasm angered her. "Are you going to listen to me or not?"

"Not."

"Fine. I might as well get dressed then. As you said, we've got a flight to catch."

Now it was her turn to stomp into the bathroom and slam the door.

Adam took care of paying for the room and loading their suitcases into the car. He waited for her outside the cabin, feeling too closed in by the antique-filled rooms where they'd shared so much last night. He couldn't believe the way things had turned out. So much for all his romantic plans. He'd wanted to surprise Julia, not shock her. It hurt him to realize that while he'd been imagining them growing old together, raising children together, Julia hadn't considered their relationship in terms of the future at all.

He knew that he should listen to her explanation, but he needed time to cool down first. At the moment he was still too angry and hurt to think coherently. Damn it, if this is what it felt like to ask a woman to marry him, then he'd remain a bachelor for life.

He'd just about calmed down enough to talk and to listen to Julia when she walked out of the cabin. But one look at her face told him that she had her icy control in place and that she was holding a grudge against him for his earlier refusal to listen. He sighed. For two adults specializing in communication, they'd sure managed to screw up this thing royally.

"I'm ready to leave if you are," she stated coolly. She wouldn't beg him to listen to her. If he wanted to stew in his own juices then let him.

"We get breakfast along with our room," he said, trying to sound polite. "They've set it up in the restaurant."

"I'm not hungry."

"Fine. We'll skip it."

"No, wait. If they've already set up our breakfast, then we should eat it, or at least try to. They've gone to all that work; they're expecting us to show up."

"And you always do what's expected, right?" he taunted her.

"I don't like letting people down," she replied quietly.

What about me? he wanted to say. What about letting me down?

Something about the look on his face made her put a tentative hand on his arm. "Adam..."

"You want to eat, fine. We'll eat."

It sounded more like he wanted her to choke on it, she thought dismally.

Julia only picked at the continental breakfast and fresh-fruit salad that had been set out for them. She wished she'd kept her mouth shut. She wished she and Adam were still in bed and that he'd never proposed to her in the first place. And from the look on his face, she was willing to bet he was probably wishing the same thing.

The opportunity to talk during the drive back to New Orleans didn't arise, because they got lost. Julia didn't have her mind on navigating. Adam didn't, either, for that matter. The result was that, after turning in the rental car, they barely arrived at the gate in time to catch their plane.

Once on board the plane, they discovered that May Ling was working on their flight.

"Hi, big brother," May Ling greeted Adam. "What brings you to New Orleans?" Catching sight of Julia, May Ling nodded knowingly. "Oh, now I see what the attraction was."

"What are you doing on this flight?" Adam asked. "I thought you had the East Coast route."

"I'm substituting for someone else. You don't have to sound so glad to see me, brother dear."

"It's not that." He gave her a smile, but it wasn't a genuine one. "I'm just in a rotten mood; forget it."

Julia felt May Ling's eyes on her and heard her unspoken accusation—are you the one who put him in a bad mood? It was me, she wanted to confess, to May Ling and the rest of the plane if it would make Adam happy. She hated hurting him—forget the fact that he'd hurt her back in equal measure. She felt bad enough as it was; she didn't need May Ling adding to the load. It only made Julia even more determined to clear this up before any more damage was done.

"Do you think we can talk now?" Julia asked Adam once the plane had taken off.

He shrugged. "Sure. Why not."

"Will you listen to me?"

"I'll listen. Understanding may be something else again."

"Okay, here goes. As I said earlier, maybe we haven't been completely honest with each other about our feelings. I didn't know how you felt about the traveling I have to do; you never said anything. In fact, sometimes I even wondered if you noticed that I was gone."

"Oh, I noticed all right." His voice was grim.

"Do you remember before I left for this trip, I said things had been getting complicated lately?"

"You also said you didn't want to talk about it," he reminded her.

"I'm ready to talk about it now. I should have talked about it then," she admitted. "Before I left for this trip, Helen called me into her office for a lecture. It wasn't very pleasant. The bottom line was that she felt I'd been slacking off, that I hadn't been devoting as much attention to my job as I should be. Maybe she was right. I haven't been putting in the hours I used to before I met you. She said I'd have to make choices, that there weren't enough hours in the day to do everything."

"And what did you say?"

"That I'd go to New Orleans. That I'd try harder. Obviously I'm not very good at juggling the responsibilities of a demanding job and a relationship. It's going to take more practice and more effort on my part."

"What about those choices that Helen told you you'd have to make?"

"I'm still working on them. I don't want to lose you, Adam. I love you. But I don't want to lose my job, either. I've worked long and hard to get where I am, and my promotion is on the line here. Besides, Helen has gone out on many a limb for me in the four years I've been with Dynamics. I owe her. She's been my mentor, and I feel guilty that I've let her down. I feel guilty that I've let you down, too."

"You want to please everyone. You always have. Haven't you learned yet that you have to please yourself first?"

"I'm trying to learn that, but it's difficult for me. And even when I do think about what pleases me, I still get into trouble. You please me. So does my job. I need both, but in different ways."

"Fine. I've got no problem with that. But we're not talking about a regular job. This one seems to require more than a normal or even a reasonable amount of devotion. You said that Helen had been your mentor. She obviously wants you to follow in her footsteps. She sees you as being similar to her. And you're not, you know. You've got a tender side, a caring side that Helen simply doesn't have. And as far as her going out on a limb for you, I don't buy that. She saw your ability, and I'll give her credit for her good judgement. But you've done the work yourself, Julia. You've made your own reputation, and it's a damn good reputation, I might add. You're one of the best in the business. Helen isn't doing you any favors. You've earned a promotion, and if you ask me, you should have received it a lot sooner than this. In my opinion Helen has been taking advantage of you."

"It sounds to me as if you feel threatened by Helen."

"Damn right I do. It feels like I'm in a tug-of-war with her, and you're in the middle. I don't like that," Adam stated.

"How do you think I feel as the one being tugged?" Julia retorted.

"So you admit that she is pulling you away from me?"

"Responsibilities and obligations are pulling me. I want to be able to handle the life I already have before taking on additional commitments."

"By handle, you mean control." He shook his head. "That day will never come. We can't control every part of our lives. Things happen. Circumstances change."

"I realize that."

"I don't think you do realize it. You're waiting for the perfect set of circumstances to happen, the perfect classroom scenario. You could be waiting forever."

Julia didn't know what to say to that, so she kept quiet. It seemed to her that the more she tried to explain, the more remote Adam became, and that panicked her. She'd never seen him this way before. Oh, she'd seen him angry, but never distant. She never realized how cool his blue eyes could be. He'd always looked at her with such warmth before.

Taking her cue from Adam, who had closed his eyes and was apparently sleeping, Julia leaned her seat back and rested. Actually she was trying to come up with a way of pleasing everyone concerned in this situation. All she ended up with was a headache.

As if sensing that something was wrong, May Ling left Julia and Adam alone for most of the trip. Adam offered to give his sister a lift into town after they landed, but she declined.

Julia shivered in the below-zero weather as she followed Adam across the airport parking garage where he'd left his car. She supposed she should have waited for him inside the terminal, as he'd suggested, but she was reluctant to let him out of her sight. Some part of her feared he might not come back to get her. She knew it was an irrational fear. Adam was too much of a gentleman to leave her stranded, and she was too experienced a traveler not to make her own way home from the airport even if he had left her. But it was a feeling she had, a sensation in the pit of her stomach, a shaky dread that was hard to put a name to and even harder to get rid of.

The heater warmed the car in no time, but Julia remained chilled in a way that had nothing to do with the outside temperature. Adam seemed perfectly happy to stay quiet. He'd even turned on the radio, a signal to her that no further discussion would occur between them.

As they got closer and closer to her apartment, she became more and more convinced that she had to get some sort of dialogue going between them. "I never realized you resented my job so much," she said.

"Maybe it's not your job as much as it's your att—"

"Don't you dare say it's my attitude," she warned him. Her nerves by now were completely frazzled. "I've had it up to here—" she gestured to a space several inches over her head "—with complaints about my attitude. First Helen and now you. You think I don't devote enough time to our relationship, and Helen thinks I don't devote enough time to my job."

"And what do you think?" he demanded.

"That you're pushing me. And I don't understand why."

"Because I see you putting up obstacles between us, and I see no sign of you even thinking about us having a future together."

"I'm not good enough at relationships for marriage yet."

He stopped the car in front of her building before turning to face her. "It takes practice and commitment."

"That's easy for you to say. There's no conflict between a relationship and a career for you."

"And there shouldn't be for you, either. You aren't sounding like a woman who loves too much. You're sounding like a woman who can't love enough, who's afraid of commitment, who won't give of herself."

His words cut her deeply, and she could feel the pain clear to her soul. "How can you say that to me?" she choked. "After all that we've shared?"

"As the song says, 'There's more to love than making love'," he told her bluntly.

"And part of love is giving the person you love the time and space that they need," she retorted.

"You can have all the space you want." He got out of the car and unloaded her suitcase.

She opened her car door before he could do it for her.

They stood on the sidewalk, the air around them as cold as the words they were exchanging.

"As for time," he said, "well, when the time comes that you get your priorities straight and figure out what it is you really want out of life—when the time comes for you to worry about pleasing yourself as much as you worry about pleasing other people—then let me know. You know where to find me. Until that time I think we'd both be better off on our own. We're only hurting each other this way, and as you said, we've done enough of that already. So I'm going to give you the thing you seem to want the most from me—my absence."

Standing there with tears in her eyes, Julia watched him drive away and died a little inside. Her worst nightmare had come true. The juggling act was over, and the shattered pieces of her life would never be the same again.

Eleven

There were many ways to be alone, and Julia experienced every one of them during the next few days. Alone in a crowd, alone at work, alone in the middle of the night when it felt as if she were the only person left on the planet. The loneliness haunted her—as did the pain, the anger, the fear, the rejection and the regrets.

It was easy to fall into her old habit of inundating herself with work; the hard part was just getting through the day without thinking of Adam. She soon learned it wasn't only hard; it was impossible. Oh, sure, sometimes she could put him out of her mind for an extra hour or two. But then *bang!* something would remind her of him—the way he smiled, the way he looked wearing his reading glasses, the way he looked wearing nothing at all. Then she'd have to work twice as hard to forget him again. Not that she could ever hope to truly forget him, but she did want to forget this awful pain, this emptiness she felt inside.

He'd left her, she told herself over and over again. Just as she'd been afraid, he'd walked out on her. The ironic thing was that he'd left because he thought she didn't love him *enough*, not that she loved him too much. She was definitely still having trouble with balance here, she told herself bitterly.

Had it been a self-fulfilling prophecy? Had she unintentionally but perhaps deliberately driven Adam away? Julia wondered what it was about her that made it so hard for her to deal with love. But she had to consider that issue alone because she had no one to talk to, no close personal friends.

She didn't feel comfortable talking to Maria about the more intimate details of her relationship with Adam. She knew Maria would probably tell her she was an idiot for refusing Adam's proposal. And after all Maria was a work associate. And she certainly didn't feel comfortable talking with Patti or her mother about her breakup with Adam. She knew that they'd only view this as another example of "Julia screwing up." She didn't even have a turtle to talk to, as she'd done at Adam's loft that New Year's Day, so long ago. It took her a moment to realize that in fact it had only been a little more than a week ago. She found it hard to believe how so much could have changed in such a short time.

One person did seem to be pleased, and that was Helen. Julia knew that her boss welcomed her renewed obsession with work. What she didn't know was why Helen had called her into her office.

"Now don't look so uneasy," Helen said. "I called you into my office this time for good news. Your promotion is in the final stages now. It's looking very good. It will mean a raise, not as large an increase as I would have liked to see you get, but then you can't have everything."

That was one thing Julia had learned.

"I have to say that I'm very pleased with the changes you've made, with your renewed enthusiasm. It's very gratifying to see," Helen stated.

Julia cynically wondered if her pain was as gratifying to see. She knew she was pale; she was living on caffeine, not getting enough sleep, existing on her nerves.

"There's a good chance that Intercorp is going to give us another assignment, this one for individual district offices. It will be even more traveling than the previous project," Helen said, "and the seminars will be geared more to entry-level managers instead of the middle managers we addressed last time. But this is a wonderful opportunity for Dynamics. And for you. Think of the experience you'd gain as a project leader on a project of this size. Of course we'd share the responsibility—it's too large a project for your first venture. You don't have the experience yet, but you will. Someday you'll be sitting in this seat."

"And where will you be sitting?" Julia asked.

Helen actually grinned. "In the president's chair. Our fearless leader will be retiring in another two years. And when that day comes, I'll be ready. Just as I want you to be ready, Julia. You've got what it takes; you can go as far as you want."

Yes, but do I really want to? Julia wondered. She lived in an age of ambition where work was supposed to matter more than pleasure, and success was more important than love. There was nothing wrong with loving her job, as long as she didn't go overboard. It suddenly hit her that maybe she'd been a woman who'd not only loved romantically too much, but also loved her job too much. Maybe she'd applied those same bad habits to her career, and instead of developing moderation, she'd simply substituted a job for a man.

"Are you all right?" Helen asked as Julia stared at her blankly.

"What kind of raise would this promotion entail?"

Helen looked a bit taken aback, and Julia knew why. She'd never been overly concerned about money before. She received a salary rather than an hourly wage, so the tremendous amount of overtime she put in was never reimbursed. It hadn't bothered her before; keeping busy had kept her from having to think about her private life. Whenever there had been a job that needed doing, Julia had done it. The company had needed her. But the need to be needed, that was part of loving too much. Why hadn't she seen it before?

"What kind of raise?" Helen repeated. "You mean the amount?"

"That's right."

Helen named a figure that was ridiculously low.

You deserve more than that, Julia thought to herself. You're too smart to be taken in by a fancy title, twice the responsibility and only a five-percent raise. "I've been working for Dynamics for four years now. I've done the work of a project leader even if I haven't had the title. My expertise is worth a lot more than that."

"Agreed, but unfortunately the company isn't in a position to offer more at this time. I wish we were."

So what was Helen offering her? Julia wondered. Twice the work load, more traveling instead of less. It sounded like a fine place to hide. She'd be too inundated with work for anything else. And Dynamics did still need her. But what was she getting in return? Not enough. It wasn't just the money. It was the obsession. She wanted more out of life. She wanted the *time* for more.

"You know if I had my way, you'd get more money," Helen was saying. "But there are plenty of opportunities involved with this position, Julia. It could be a stepping stone to bigger and better things for you. A few years as project leader, and you could move up to a vice presidency. As you know, I've considered myself to be your mentor since you came to Dynamics. If I haven't said it before, I'm very proud of you. Proud of the way you've conducted yourself, always getting the job done."

Julia felt the threat of tears. Was this what she'd been waiting for? Approval? For someone to say they were proud of her, that she'd done a good job. Someone to give her legitimacy as a person, someone to say *yes, you are worthy*.

The tears rolled down her cheeks.

Helen looked at Julia in horror. "What's wrong? Are you sick?"

Julia shook her head, unable to speak.

Helen got up and handed her some Kleenex before awkwardly patting her on the shoulder. "Maybe you'd better tell me what's going on."

"This isn't going to work." Julia hurriedly wiped her tears away.

"What isn't?"

"I know you're trying to be helpful, and I appreciate all you've done for me, really I do. But there's more to life than just work. I want there to be more to my life than just work."

Helen frowned. "This doesn't sound like you, Julia. You've always asked for more work, never complained about overtime. At least not until..."

Julia supplied the answer before Helen did. "Until Adam."

"Is he the reason for this sudden turnaround, for your crying jag?"

"No. I'm the reason. This is my decision. You told me not long ago that I'd have to make some difficult choices. You were right. I've made mistakes, but I know what I want now. And I don't want to be obsessed with work."

"Why not? What's wrong with that?"

"Nothing maybe, for you. But it's not right for me anymore."

"You're just feeling depressed. Give it some time," Helen advised. "You'll see things differently tomorrow."

"No, I won't."

Seeing the determined look in Julia's eyes, Helen quietly said, "No, maybe you won't. You're serious about this, aren't you? I don't get it," she said bluntly. "One minute we're talking about your promotion, and the next minute you're telling me that this won't work. It must be the money. You're upset with the low raise. Is that it?"

Julia shook her head. "It's about needing approval, about trying to please everyone else and not knowing how to please myself. I think today's been a long time coming." Maybe since I was five and wanted approval from my mother, wanted to please her, Julia thought to herself with growing insight. "I'm not like you, Helen. I thought I was. But I was kidding myself."

Helen perched on the corner of her desk and gave Julia a curiously resigned look. "You know, in some sort of strange way, I was afraid this day would come. I was kidding myself, too. Maybe I was trying to make you into my own image, seeing myself in you, thinking we were so alike. Oh, you're determined all right. You've even been driven on occasion. But you're a softy underneath all that efficiency."

"I know." Julia was surprised that Helen had noticed that, though.

"Look, I've got one more piece of advice to offer you. Check out..." Helen mentioned the name of one of the largest accounting firms in Chicago. "I happen to know they're looking for an in-house efficiency instructor for their business-management department."

Julia was even more surprised now. "Why are you telling me this?"

"Because I'm sure you could get the job if you applied for it. The salary is higher than anything we can offer you, and the stability is what I think you're looking for."

"I don't know what to say."

"Don't say anything. And if you tell anyone that we've had this conversation, I'll deny it. It wouldn't do for me to ruin my reputation for being hard as nails, let alone telling one of my best instructors about a job elsewhere." Helen shook her head. "I hate to see you go. Dynamics will miss you. If I were a better manager I'd convince you to stay."

"You couldn't do that."

"Not even with a larger raise?"

"No. It isn't the money. I want more freedom. I don't want to be a slave to my job any longer. I've hidden here long enough. It's time I moved on." Before leaving her office, Julia paused at the door and softly added, "I think underneath it all, you're something of a softy, too, Helen. Thanks."

Julia was tempted to call Adam right away and tell him about the changes she was making in her life. But she waited, wanting things to be a little more settled before she went to him. This transitional time was for her own benefit.

Julia was interviewed by the huge accounting firm Helen had told her about and was immediately offered the position. Two weeks later, after a farewell party at Dynamics, where rumor had it that Helen's eyes had actually misted, Julia began her new life.

Like a caterpillar that was finally coming out of its protective cocoon, Julia had finally accepted who she was and what she wanted. She replaced her blend-into-the-background suits with here-I-am clothes—long, lean jackets in vivid jewel tones: red, brilliant blue, even purple. She hung her Monet poster on her wall over her couch. And she phoned home and had a long talk with her mother. Then she called Patti.

"I called you on your birthday," Patti said. "That was almost three weeks ago. I left a message on your machine. I suppose you were out of town on some trip again. You do too much traveling."

"You're right. That's one of the reasons I quit."

"You what?!" Patti couldn't have sounded more shocked if Julia had announced she was moving to Mars.

"I quit."

"Is this some sort of mid-life crisis or something?"

"I'm only thirty, Patti. Age had nothing to do with it, unless you consider the fact that I got a little wiser as well as getting a little older."

"I don't understand. This doesn't sound like you at all," Patti said. "Does Mom know?"

"Yes. I just talked to her."

"What did she say?"

"A lot of things." To Julia the most important had been that her mother was pleased for her. "It's about time you did something for yourself," her mother had told her. "You do entirely too much for other people. Even as a little girl you were always trying to make things better for everyone. I used to worry about it. I hoped you'd find someone who'd do for you the way you've always done for others. Adam seemed like that kind of man. I want you to be happy, baby. I may not say it very often, but I do love you, you know."

"Julia, are you still there?" Patti demanded. "What's really going on?"

"I told you. I quit my job at Dynamics."

"Are you out of work, in trouble, what?"

"Thanks for the vote of confidence, Patti," Julia noted dryly.

"You've got enough confidence of your own; you don't need more from me."

"Maybe I do," Julia said quietly. "Did you ever consider the possibility that I'm not as sure of myself as I may seem?"

"No," Patti said just as quietly. "I never considered that possibility. You've always been so sure of where you're going. I always envied that in you. You never hesitate over anything."

Julia didn't know whether to laugh or cry. "Oh, Patti, I hesitate all the time. I just don't show it. And as far as envy goes, *I've* always envied *you*."

"What on earth for?"

"Because you're able to get along with people so well. Things seem to come so easily for you. You always seemed to breeze through life while I was continually stumbling along."

"You mean all the time I was envying you, you were envying me?" Patti demanded.

"Yes. Pretty dumb, huh?" Julia said.

"Real dumb. How come we never talked this way before?"

"At least we're talking this way now," Julia replied. "It may have taken me a while, but I think I've got a better handle on my life now. I know what I want."

"And is Adam what you want?" Patti asked.

"Yes."

"Then he'd better watch out. Go get him, sis!"

"I will."

Knowing Adam's predilection for grand gestures, Julia felt that a mere phone call wasn't enough. She wanted to make a statement. So here she was, standing in her bulky winter coat outside Adam's classroom, trying to get the nerve to go in and interrupt his four o'clock class on mastering creativity. She still wasn't sure of her exact game plan yet; she had several options in mind.

Telling herself this was no time to chicken out, she took her courage in hand and opened the door. She already knew the layout of the room; she'd been here before in happier times with Adam. She planned on getting those happy times back again.

The door opened into the back of the large classroom, which had a center aisle leading down to the podium where Adam was speaking. From the few sentences she heard, she realized he was planning on doing his favorite barrier-breaking exercise, using sentences beginning with *I* or *My*.

When he said, "I need a volunteer," she couldn't have asked for a more perfect opening.

Several lovely coeds raised their hands eagerly, so Julia moved quickly. "I'd like to volunteer to be your partner," she announced.

Everyone turned around to look at her, but Julia only had eyes for Adam. Was he pleased to see her? He looked pale. Was he angry? Had he been ill? Then he smiled, and her fears melted like snow in a spring thaw. She knew then that everything was going to be all right. And that knowledge gave her the confidence to continue with her plan.

"Come on down," he invited her.

She joined him in the front of the classroom.

Adam didn't take his eyes off her as he instructed the class to begin the timed exercise. The ensuing noise of fifty voices all speaking at once ensured that they wouldn't be overheard.

Julia began.

"I missed you," she said softly.

"I missed you, too."

"I love you."

"I love you, too."

"I know what I want now. I want you."

"I'm glad."

"I only have one more thing to say."

"I'm all ears."

"I'm not wearing anything under this coat."

Adam froze. "Nothing at all?"

She shook her head.

"Class dismissed!" he shouted.

The students, who weren't about to question the early break, dispersed quickly. But not as quickly as Adam hustled Julia from that classroom.

"You always told me I should be more creative. Was that creative enough for you?" she inquired with a grin.

He steered her around a group of milling students. "As soon as I get you alone, I'll show you creativity," he muttered.

"Professor MacKenzie," an authoritative voice called out. "Professor MacKenzie!"

Adam reluctantly stopped. He didn't have much choice. The professor who'd called his name was blocking the hallway. Adam cursed his luck. Why now? Why did he have to run into Professor Norman "Stickler-for-Propriety" Pinkerton now?

"Professor MacKenzie, don't you have a class to give?" Professor Pinkerton said.

"We finished early," Adam replied curtly.

But Professor Pinkerton didn't know how to say anything curtly. He went on and on like the stodgy windbag he was.

Meanwhile Julia unbuttoned the top button of her coat and began languidly waving her face with her hand. "It's warm in here, don't you think?" She undid another button and then another.

Without further ado, Adam cut off the loquacious professor midword and rushed Julia out of there so fast her head spun.

The drive from the campus to Adam's loft normally took twenty minutes. He made it in ten.

"Why yes, Adam, I'd love to come up to your loft and talk with you," Julia murmured wryly. "Thanks for asking me."

"I can't believe you did this," he said as he closed the door behind them.

"Are you upset?"

He took her in his arms. "After not seeing you for almost three weeks, I'm surprised I'm even halfway coherent."

"I know." She kissed his lips, his chin, his jaw, any place she could reach. "I feel the same way."

"Then why didn't you call me?"

She leaned away and unbuttoned his shirt. It seemed only fair since he was already unbuttoning her coat. "I wanted to surprise you."

"You sure did that, all right." He peeled the coat off her shoulders and let it fall to the floor. "I thought you said you weren't wearing anything under this."

"Well, it is February, Adam. I didn't want to freeze. Besides a red silk teddy doesn't really count."

"I like the garters though. Nice touch," he said appreciatively.

"I said I wanted to surprise you," she murmured as she tossed his shirt to one side. "Actually I wanted to knock your socks off. Did I?"

"Absolutely." He kicked off his shoes, peeled off his socks and tossed them over his shoulder. "Couldn't you tell?"

She shook her head. "I was too nervous."

"You didn't look very nervous to me."

"No?" She looked up from the leather belt she was unbuckling at his waist. "How did I look?"

"Sexy as hell. Like a sight for sore eyes...and other parts of my body, like my heart and soul. Oh, honey, I missed you so much."

Their kiss marked the beginning of the end. As had always been the case with them, their passion flared quickly and burned heatedly.

"We should talk first," Adam felt compelled to mutter even as he led her to the bed.

"We should," she agreed. "But let's not. We can do that later."

"Perhaps we should continue with our barrier-breaking exercise," he suggested with a rakish grin. "This is one barrier that will have to go." He swiftly removed her teddy.

"And this is another barrier that can't stay," she replied as she removed his briefs.

When she cupped him in her loving hands, he shuddered. "I can't take much more of this," he warned her in a husky growl.

"Neither can I," she admitted.

"Good."

The time for playful teasing was over. Locked together, bare skin pressed against heated flesh, they shared a kiss that was both demanding and giving.

Adam caressed her, running his hands up and down her back, as if to reassure himself that she was really there with him and that this wasn't a dream. Julia did the same.

"I want to go slow," Adam muttered. "But I want you so much I don't think I can."

"I don't want you to go slow." She arched against him, her movements reinforcing her words. "I want you with me now."

"Now?" His hand closed over her breast with blatant possessiveness. "Are you sure?"

"I'm positive," she murmured as pleasure sizzled from the sensitive tips of her breasts down to the spot that ached for his touch.

He smiled and whispered, "Maybe I should do this first...."

She cried out with excitement as he touched her intimately, lovingly.

"Yes. Yes, do that first...."

"And then this..." He rolled away to reach into the drawer of the bedside table. A moment later he returned and resumed his heated seduction, his fingers driving her to higher and higher planes of ecstasy.

Just as the final pleasure seized her, Adam finally came to her, completing their union. For Julia the spiraling trip began again, only this time Adam was with her every step of the way—the heated tautness, the rippling convulsions, the joyful release.

In the warm afterglow of their lovemaking, Julia rested her head on his shoulder and gently ran her hand back and forth over his chest. It was a gesture that spoke of tenderness, of caring.

"I've got so much to tell you," Julia said.

He kissed the top of her head. "Just tell me you love me and will never leave me again."

"I didn't leave you in the first place. You were the one who walked away."

"I must have been an idiot."

"Not really." As Julia told him about the changes she'd made in her life, about the insights she'd gained, she watched the pride and admiration grow on his face.

"Do you have any regrets about leaving Dynamics?" he asked her.

"None. I did what was right. I knew it at the time, and I know it even more now. I'm sorry for making things so difficult for you. I want you to know that you're never going to have to go through anything like that again," she promised him.

"Anything like what?"

"Proposing," she said bluntly.

Adam's heart sank. Was Julia still against the idea of marriage? Had she progressed so far only to still be gun-shy of the final commitment?

He would have spoken, but she put her fingers to his lips and shook her head. "I'm not finished yet. I have one more thing to say. Actually, it's a question. Adam MacKenzie, will you marry me?" She grinned at his startled expression. "Really, Adam, there's no need to look so surprised. I love you; you love me. Marriage isn't that radical a suggestion." Her grin widened as she deliberately recited his own words back to him. "Well? What's your answer?"

He reached over and opened the drawer of the bedside table. This time he came back with a small jeweler's box in his hand. "The answer is yes." He removed a pearl-and-garnet engagement ring from the box and slid it onto her finger.

"Does that mean it's official?" she asked shakily.

"It means we've still got time for a Valentine's Day wedding."

"Why, Adam, I do believe you're right," she said demurely. "There's a very good chance you might get your way, after all." Which was fine with her because Adam's way had turned out to be her way as well—the way of love.

* * * * *

ANOTHER BRIDE FOR A BRANIGAN BROTHER!

Branigan's Touch
by Leslie Davis Guccione

Available in October 1989

You've written in asking for more about the Branigan brothers,
so we decided to give you Jody's story—from *his* perspective.

Look for Mr. October—*Branigan's Touch*—a *Man of the Month*,
coming from Silhouette Desire.

Following #311 *Bittersweet Harvest*, #353 *Still Waters* and #376
Something in Common, *Branigan's Touch* still stands on its
own. You'll enjoy the warmth and charm of the Branigan clan—
and watch the sparks fly when another Branigan man meets his
match with an O'Connor woman!

SD523-1

Silhouette Romance®

AWARD OF EXCELLENCE

LONG, TALL TEXANS

Diana Palmer brings you the second Award of Excellence title

SUTTON'S WAY

In Diana Palmer's bestselling Long, Tall Texans trilogy, you had a mesmerizing glimpse of Quinn Sutton—a mean, lean Wyoming wildcat of a man, with a disposition to match.

Now, in September, Quinn's back with a story of his own. Set in the Wyoming wilderness, he learns a few things about women from snowbound beauty Amanda Callaway—and a lot more about love.

He's a Texan at heart . . . who soon has a Wyoming wedding in mind!

The Award of Excellence is given to one specially selected title per month. Spend September discovering *Sutton's Way* #670 . . . only in Silhouette Romance.

RS670-1R

Silhouette Intimate Moments®

COMING IN OCTOBER!
A FRESH LOOK FOR
Silhouette Intimate Moments!

Silhouette Intimate Moments has always brought you the perfect combination of love and excitement, and now they're about to get a new cover design that's just as exciting as the stories inside.

Over the years we've brought you stories that combined romance with something a little bit different, like adventure or suspense. We've brought you longtime favorite authors like Nora Roberts and Linda Howard. We've brought you exciting new talents like Patricia Gardner Evans and Marilyn Pappano. Now let us bring you a new cover design guaranteed to catch your eye just as our heroes and heroines catch your heart.

Look for it in October—
Only from Silhouette Intimate Moments!

You'll flip . . . your pages won't!
Read paperbacks *hands-free* with

Book Mate • I

The perfect "mate" for all your romance paperbacks

Traveling • Vacationing • At Work • In Bed • Studying • Cooking • Eating

Perfect size for all standard paperbacks, this wonderful invention makes reading a pure pleasure! Ingenious design holds paperback books OPEN and FLAT so even wind can't ruffle pages — leaves your hands free to do other things. Reinforced, wipe-clean vinyl-covered holder flexes to let you turn pages without undoing the strap . . . supports paperbacks so well, they have the strength of hardcovers!

Pages turn WITHOUT opening the strap

SEE-THROUGH STRAP

Reinforced back stays flat.

Built in bookmark

BOOK MARK

BACK COVER HOLDING STRIP

10" x 7¼" opened.
Snaps closed for easy carrying, too

COMING SOON...

Indulge a Little
Give a Lot

An irresistible opportunity to pamper
yourself with free* gifts and help a
great cause, Big Brothers/Big Sisters
Programs and Services.

*With proofs-of-purchase plus postage and handling.

Watch for it in October!

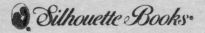

Harlequin Books®

Silhouette Books®